THE TOTALLY
AWESOME
WORLD OF

CAITLIN CLARK

LEARN ALL THERE IS TO KNOW ABOUT YOUR FAVORITE ALL-STAR

—

SARA WEISS

becker&mayer! kids

CONTENTS

INTRODUCTION

—

One rainy evening in May, Caitlin Clark and her teammates gathered in a tunnel inside the Gainbridge Fieldhouse, waiting to make their grand entrance onto the basketball court. Caitlin was about to play her very first home preseason game in the WNBA at the Fieldhouse, the home of the Indiana Fever. It was a dream come true.

As the crowd cheered and the announcer called out Caitlin's teammates, the players ran out one by one.

"Now, from Iowa," the announcer said, "Number 22 . . . Caitlin Claaaark!"

The crowd went wild as Caitlin ran out to greet them.

As a little kid, she had acted out a scene like this one so many times, bursting from the hall closet in uniform, her mom announcing her while an imaginary crowd roared. Now here she was. Music blared, and Freddie Fever, the big-eyed, orange-and-blue mascot of the Indiana Fever, started dancing and pumping up the crowd.

There was a sea of fans in the stands dressed in Fever colors—navy blue, red, and gold—and holding up signs with Caitlin's number or messages like, "You Inspire Me, #22," "When I Grow Up, I Wanna Be Like Clark," and "Welcome to Indy, Caitlin!" Kids were screaming her name and holding out programs, basketballs, jerseys, posters, and sneakers for her to sign.

Caitlin absolutely wanted to win this game against the Atlanta Dream, but no matter what the outcome, she planned to stay and sign as many autographs as she could. The kids in the stadium didn't only care how many points she scored or whether she won or lost. They were just happy to see their favorite player, and it meant everything to Caitlin to be able to give them that.

Caitlin knew exactly what it was like to be that kid in the stands holding out a jersey, hoping for a chance to get an autograph or even just to make eye contact with one of her heroes. She wouldn't be on that court if it weren't for the athletes who had inspired her. Her role models had helped her believe that with big dreams and hard work, she could be whoever she wanted to be.

And it had taken *so much* hard work to get here. How many hours had she spent shooting hoops in her driveway and in the gym before and after team practices? Now, she shot more than 300 baskets a day, a mix of three-pointers, midrange shots, and free throws. There were sprints, squats, jumps, weights, dead lifts, and lunges. There were hours upon hours of dribbling drills—crossovers, in and out double cross, and one-handed and behind-the-back dribbles from half court and back. She practiced the routine tirelessly to make it feel like second nature, so that when she got onto the court with her team at game time, she felt comfortable and confident. The goal was to make it look effortless.

Caitlin loved to see how the women's game had changed in the years since she'd started playing in college. Ticket sales to get into the games were at an all-time high. Over 19 million people had watched the NCAA Championship game during Caitlin's senior year of college, when her team, the Iowa Hawkeyes, played the South Carolina Gamecocks. It was the most watched basketball game in years, beating not just other games in the women's NCAA tournament but also the men's college tournament and even the pros! There were thirteen *thousand* fans in attendance for her first game, a sold-out arena, triple the size of the crowd of the previous season's first home game.

Not too long before, only men's basketball had been televised on major networks and brought in massive crowds like this. With Caitlin's rise to fame, all that changed. Her successes brought in new fans, helped sell thousands of tickets (and millions of jerseys, T-shirts, shoes, and posters), and sparked important conversations about fairness and equality in sports. The outsized impact she's had on sports and society has been called "The Caitlin Clark Effect."

Fans traveled from far away, waiting in long lines to see her shoot her signature "logos," or long three-pointers, which she seemed to launch miles away from the basket. They came to see the way she passed the ball too. As the point guard, she orchestrated the team's tempo and tactics, using her unique ability to quickly read a situation and execute flawless plays to find opportunities that others couldn't. She kept the ball moving and flummoxed her opponents, performing behind-the-back or no-look passes to her teammates that tripped up defenders and set up her team to score.

Throughout her time playing in college, Caitlin had set a huge number of records, including becoming the all-time highest-scoring player in Division I college basketball in history, more than any other female or male player. People called her a "generational talent," or the kind of talent that comes around only once every 20 years or so. While Caitlin was proud of what she had accomplished, it wasn't only about setting records and winning awards for her. Basketball is a team sport, and she wanted her team to win a championship.

Today, at just 22 years old, she carries a lot of pressure on her shoulders as a WNBA rookie. The game is faster and much more physical than college basketball.

While Caitlin is of average height for a point guard at 6 feet tall, she doesn't have the bulk and muscle that many other players have. Going into her first professional game, she knew there was going to be so much to learn. While there were clearly so many fans rooting for her, there were haters too. Some people were expecting her to fail.

That had never stopped her before, though, and it wasn't going to stop her now. Caitlin had been a competitive athlete since she was old enough to hold a basketball, and over the years, she had faced plenty of challenges and learned how to both handle losses and manage her expectations. No matter what hardships she faced, she knew she had the drive and determination to pick herself back up. She was ready to prove that she belonged here.

She and her teammates formed a huddle with their arms around each other, swaying side to side. Then they brought their hands together in the middle for a group cheer. Caitlin and her teammates took the floor, setting up in position for tip-off. The ref tossed the ball up at center court, and Fever forward NaLyssa Smith got her hand on it before her opponent, sending it right to Caitlin. Caitlin took the first dribble of the game, keeping her eyes up and scanning the floor, mapping out the position of her teammates and defenders. She sent a one-handed overhead pass that landed right back into NaLyssa's hands to get the play started.

Caitlin was more than ready for this moment. Game on.

CHAPTER

GROWING UP
IN IOWA

EARLY
DREAMS

Caitlin Clark wrote down her future dreams** on a piece of paper for a third-grade assignment: *To travel across the whole world,* she wrote inside a little cloud bubble. *To have two Bernese mountain dogs. To meet Maya Moore. To go [to college] on a basketball scholarship.* Number one on the list, written twice, was, *To be in the WNBA.*

Who Is
Maya Moore?

Caitlin Clark's role model, Maya Moore, is a former professional basketball player and American social justice advocate. *Sports Illustrated* called her the "greatest winner in the history of women's basketball." She was selected for the Women's Basketball Hall of Fame in 2024.

Maya played forward for the University of Connecticut women's basketball team, the most successful women's basketball program in the United States. She won back-to-back national championships with UConn in 2009 and 2010. She was then the first overall pick in the 2011 WNBA Draft and joined the Minnesota Lynx. In 2012 and 2016, Maya played on the US Olympic team, winning gold both years. She is one of only 11 women ever to earn an Olympic gold medal, an NCAA Championship, a FIBA World Cup gold, and a WNBA Championship.

What Is the WNBA?

The Women's National Basketball Association (WNBA) is a women's professional basketball league based in the United States. The league was founded in 1996 as the women's counterpart to the National Basketball Association (NBA). There are 12 teams that play regular games from May to September, with an All-Star Game in July. The league is split into two conferences with six teams each. The Eastern Conference includes the Atlanta Dream, Chicago Sky, Connecticut Sun, Indiana Fever, New York Liberty, and Washington Mystics, while the Western Conference has the Dallas Wings, Las Vegas Aces, Los Angeles Sparks, Minnesota Lynx, Phoenix Mercury, and Seattle Storm.

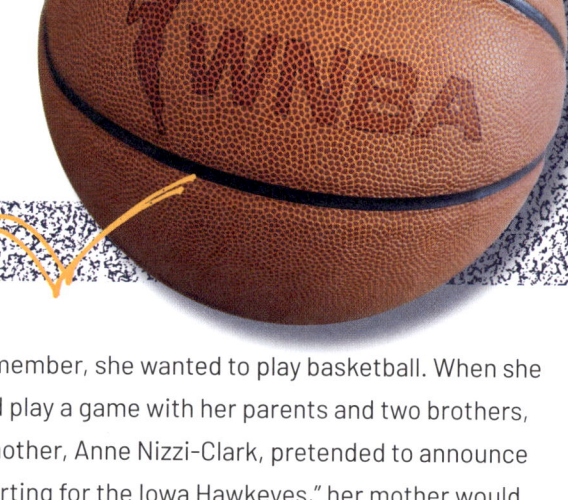

For as long as Caitlin could remember, she wanted to play basketball. When she was just three years old, she would play a game with her parents and two brothers, hiding in the mudroom while her mother, Anne Nizzi-Clark, pretended to announce the lineup for a big game. "Now starting for the Iowa Hawkeyes," her mother would say, "Caity Claaaaark!" Caitlin would burst through the door sporting a Hawkeyes jersey and a football helmet, doing a lap around the living room as if it were a packed arena.

At five years old, Caitlin played on boys' basketball teams with her brothers, dribbling down the court and making layups. She had gotten good by shooting baskets in her family's driveway, backing up more and more, her shooting range getting longer and longer, until her dad had to pave over a patch of grass to make the home court even bigger.

FAMILY
LIFE

aitlin was born in Des Moines, Iowa, on January 22, 2002. The date of her birth would become an important number: number 22. It was the number she would wear on her jersey when she got older and played in front of tens of thousands of fans.

Caitlin wasn't the only athletic one in her family, though. Her father, Brent Clark, had played basketball and baseball at Simpson College, earning all-conference honors in both sports. He was also Caitlin's first basketball coach. He pushed her to work on the basics, making sure she had the right technique and form before letting her throw three-pointers. At the time, Caitlin felt that he was slowing her down. "I was mad at him about it," she told ESPN, "but looking back, shooting form fundamentals are the best thing." Playing basketball in the gym with her dad was one of her favorite things to do. She would shoot and he would catch her rebounds.

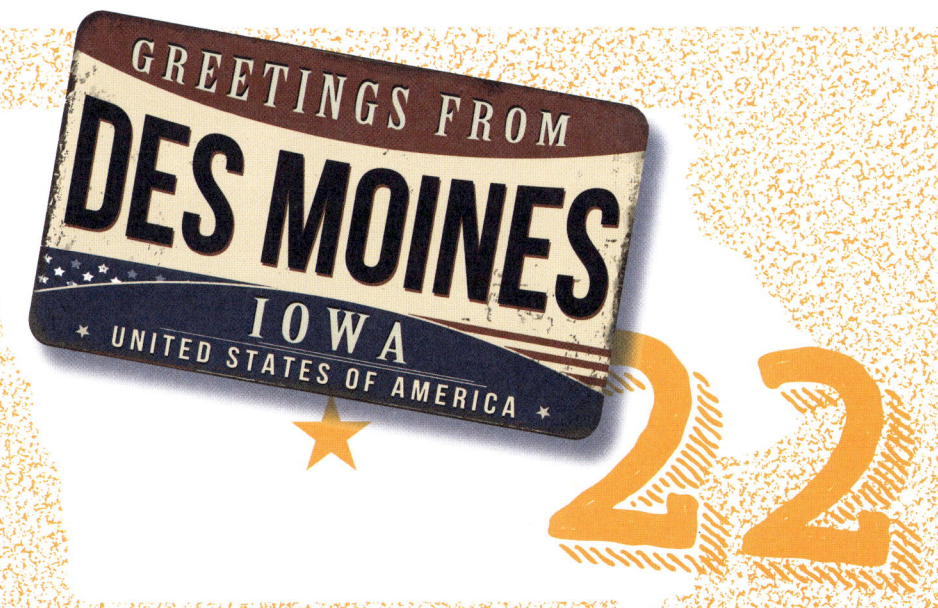

Her father could tell, even when she was as young as four years old, that she had a rare talent. "I don't recall that she would ever miss a shot," he told Iowa TV station KCRG. "The baskets were at 5 or 6 feet (1.5 or 1.8 m). She would just pull up from the free throw line and swish. She could also really handle the ball at that age."

Caitlin's mother, Anne, was also raised around sports. Anne's father, Bob Nizzi, was the football coach at the high school Caitlin and her two brothers attended, Dowling Catholic High School in West Des Moines. And Caitlin's two brothers, Blake and Colin, played every sport imaginable too.

Their family life revolved around athletics. Anne supported her children's love of sports, cheering them on from the sidelines, fostering their competitive sides, and helping them to find their true sparks. They would go watch college basketball games at nearby Drake University and sometimes drive more than three hours to Minneapolis just so Caitlin could watch her idol, WNBA player Maya Moore, play with the Minnesota Lynx. One time, fans were allowed to come onto the court after a game to meet the players, and Caitlin, who couldn't stop herself from fangirling, just ran up and gave Maya Moore a hug.

That moment would always stay in Caitlin's mind. Now that she is a superstar herself, Caitlin tries to be present and kind to the kids who crowd around her for autographs. "I just try to take as much time as I can for those young girls," she told *USA Today*, "because Maya was so nice to me when I ran up to her, and that's something that's stuck with me."

PIONEERS

It's important to remember the legends who paved the way for Caitlin and today's other great players. Many of them did not have the same opportunities that women's basketball players now experience—but without them, the sport as we know it would not exist.

- **Pearl Moore** (played 1975–1981) set a scoring standard that stood for 45 years. In the days before women's basketball was part of the NCAA, she was a standout at Francis Marion University, averaging more than 30 points every game, every season, and ending her college career with 3,884 points. Even more impressive, she scored those points in the days before college basketball adopted the three-point shot! She then played in the short-lived Women's Basketball League, a professional league that predated the WNBA, then became a coach when the WBL went out of business.

- **Lisa Leslie** (played 1997–2009) was the first woman ever to dunk in a WNBA game. She was a four-time Olympic gold medalist and a three-time WNBA MVP, playing primarily for the Los Angeles Sparks. She was a pioneer off the court, too, building on her WNBA fame to become a model, actress, and TV sports commentator.

- **Sheryl Swoopes** (played 1997–2011) was the first player to be signed in the WNBA, a three-time WNBA MVP, and a key figure in the Houston Comets' four consecutive championships. She was a six-time All-Star and one of the all-time greats. In 2005, she made headlines by becoming one of the most high-profile professional athletes to publicly come out as LGBTQ.

- **Tamika Catchings** (played 2001–2016) played her entire 15-year career for the Indiana Fever. She is one of only 11 women ever to have received an Olympic gold medal, an NCAA Championship, a FIBA World Cup gold, and a WNBA Championship. She is also an important advocate for her fellow players, serving as president of the WNBA players association.

- **Diana Taurasi** (played 2004–present) is one of Caitlin Clark's idols. Famous for her scoring ability, clutch performances, and longevity, Taurasi has multiple WNBA scoring titles and is a three-time Olympic gold medalist. In a time when the average pro basketball career is less than 5 years, Diana has now played for 20, and in 2024 she was named a WNBA All-Star at the age of 42.

COMPETITIVE
SPIRIT

When she was little, Caitlin tried to keep up with her older brother, Blake, and his friends, whether they were playing basketball, baseball, or just running around the yard. She looked up to Blake more than anything. "He just really outworked people," Caitlin told the *Gazette*, "and I think that's kind of what I admire about him and what drove me when I was young."

But Blake and his friends were bigger and stronger than her. When she couldn't keep up or they picked on her, she got so mad that she would run inside and slam the door, red-faced and fuming. Caitlin's mother comforted her and also gave her some tough love. "If you want to play with them," Anne told her daughter, "you've got to find a way to hold your own. You're the one that wants to hang out with them and play sports with them. That's just how it's going to be."

The thing is, Caitlin *hated* losing, whether it was a board game or a sporting event. When Caitlin lost, she would get so mad at herself that tears would well up in her eyes.

Her competitiveness sometimes got in her way. She would get angry with her little brother, Colin, if he won something even as small as a **NERF fight**. Her anger sometimes got her in trouble at school too. Her PE teacher once called a meeting with her parents to talk about her outbursts when she didn't perform well in dodgeball or whatever group activity they were doing that day.

The reason Caitlin got so angry when she lost was because she cared so intensely about whatever it was she had set her mind to. "She wanted to be the best," one of her elementary school teachers

Keeping Your COOL

Especially when she was younger, Caitlin found it very frustrating to lose. Do you know the feeling? Here are three tips for cooling down:

1. **See how your body feels:** When you're mad, does your head feel dizzy? Does your heart beat fast? Do you clench your fists? If you can start to notice the signs in your body as they are happening, you can learn to manage the anger.

2. **Notice what upset you:** Were you hungry? Tired? Feeling out of control? Do transitions from doing one thing to another set you off? Were you doing something that felt too challenging? If you can understand the triggers or things that make you feel frustrated, you'll know how to prepare your body and mind for those times.

3. **Breathe deep:** Learning to breathe in and out nice and slowly is one of the best ways to help your mind and body calm down. Count to three as you breathe in, count to four as you breathe out, and repeat.

at St. Francis of Assisi recalled in an interview with *IndyStar*. "Not just do her best, but be the best."

When she figured out how to harness it, this fire and drive inside of her was also a superpower.

Caitlin's grandfather, Bob Nizzi, remembers seeing his granddaughter on the basketball court at only five years old, playing against a boy who was much bigger than her. The boy was getting in her face, fouling, and being too rough. Caitlin got mad and started to cry. Her dad, who was the coach, took her out of the game to cool off on the sidelines. He sat her down and told her calmly, "When you're ready, I'll put you back in."

Her grandfather recalls a fiery Caitlin getting back in the game and playing her hardest defense, her mind set on stopping the boy from touching that ball. "She rolled this kid out of bounds and stood over him," he said. "She's a five-year-old little girl. That is when her grandmother and I looked at each other and said, 'She's going to be really something.'"

Caitlin was used to playing on the same sports teams as her brothers and running around with the boys at recess. Her parents continued to sign her up for boys' teams all the way through sixth grade because they felt that the girls' leagues in her age group weren't challenging enough for her.

"I was always around boys that pushed me and wanted to play sports," Caitlin told ESPN. "I think it was superspecial in my development, and also it was never something that ever fazed me. It was just, like, I'm a girl. I can hold my own."

SCHOOL SPORTS

In middle school, Caitlin played a bunch of sports: soccer, basketball, softball, and track. By the time she got to high school, she narrowed it down to her two favorites—basketball and soccer—and she excelled in both.

Basketball was always on her mind, though. Her soccer teammates once caught her shooting hoops in the gym, drenched in sweat, before a big match. "They just couldn't believe that I wanted to go and work out before I had to go run around a soccer field for 90 minutes," Caitlin remembered later in an ESPN interview. After her sophomore year of high school, it became clear to Caitlin that she wanted to devote all her time and energy to basketball.

Word had started to get around about this star player before she even started high school. Her high school coach, Kristin Meyer, had heard buzz about the "stud eighth grader" coming up to the high school and was looking forward to having a good player. She watched Caitlin's club team play and thought to herself, *Oh, she's real good.*

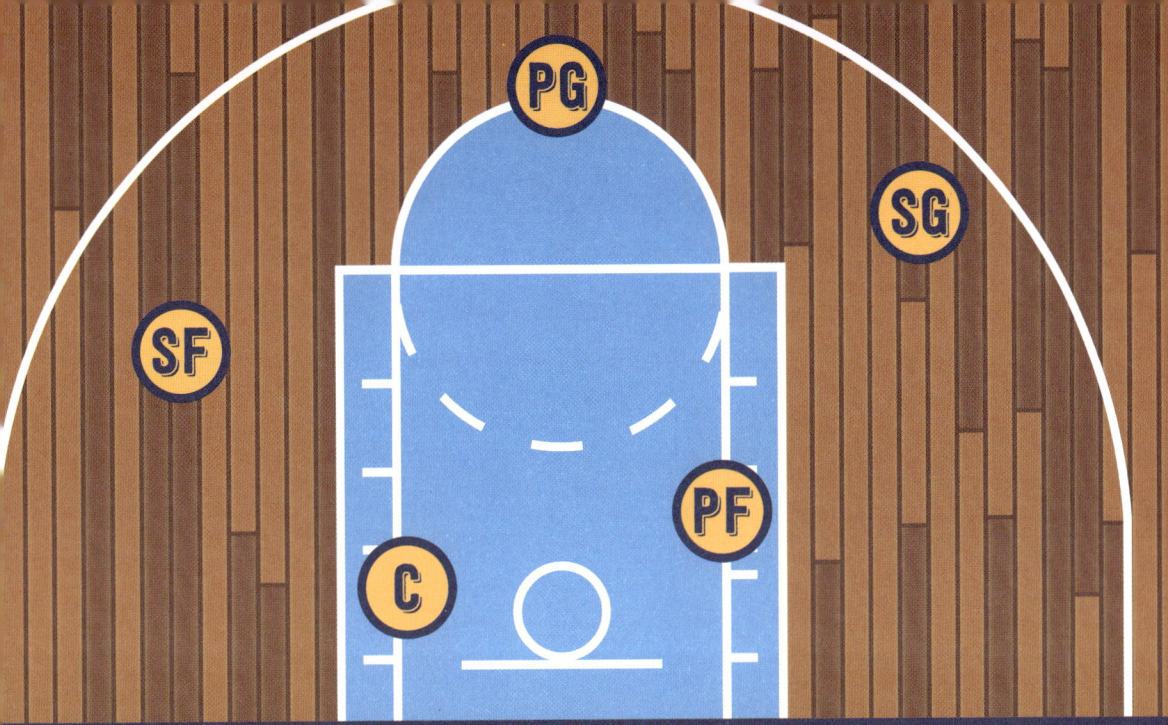

Positions on the Court

A basketball team has five players: two forwards, two guards, and a center.

Point guards (PG) manage the team's offense, moving the ball down the court and orchestrating offensive plays. They should have quick decision-making and strong ball-handling skills, and they are sometimes referred to as the "leader" or "commander" of the court.

Shooting guards (SG) operate around the perimeter, getting ready to take open shots. They should be great shooters, skilled at ball-handling and dribbling, and able to drive to the basket.

Small forwards (SF), usually taller than the guards, are often the most flexible players, able to shoot from around the perimeter but also tall enough to play nearer to the basket. They should be a well-rounded player, able to shoot, rebound, and move the ball.

Power forwards (PF) primarily operate near the basket. They should be able to move around the basket, catching rebounds, and taking short jumpers, as well as playing a key role on defense.

Centers (C), usually the tallest on the team, operate near the basket. They are responsible for setting screens (blocking moves in which a player stands by a defender to help free up a teammate), catching rebounds, and taking short jumpers.

Jan Jensen, who was the associate head coach of the University of Iowa's women's basketball team and a recruiter, heard about Caitlin when she was only in sixth grade. A year later, Coach Jensen went to West Des Moines to see Caitlin play. Within a minute of watching her, the coach knew that Caitlin had something special. "You could just tell. They're easy to identify but really hard to get," she told AP News. "Everybody can see the true, true ones. The trick is to get them." She was going to do what it took to recruit Caitlin to the University of Iowa.

Though Caitlin's high school team never won a state title, she scored 2,547 points while she was there. She averaged 32.6 points per game when she was a junior. In her most incredible high school game, Caitlin scored a whopping 60 points against Mason City, nearly breaking a state record. At the end of the game, the Mason City fans lined up to get her autograph. They could tell this star player was bound for great things.

What Does It Mean to Be
Recruited?

College athletics programs in the United States use a recruiting process to find promising athletes in high schools across the country who might want to join their college teams. They watch highlight videos, review stats, and sometimes visit schools to watch talented students play. They might also set up conversations with the student, their family, and their coach. When considering who to invite to the program, colleges are interested in the student's academics as well as their athletic ability. For the students in this process, the ultimate goal is to land an athletic scholarship that will allow them to attain a college education for free while continuing to play the game they love . . . and for a very lucky few, they might even have the chance to go pro after college.

CHAPTER

ROOKIE YEAR

CHOOSING
IOWA

While she was in high school, recruiters from different colleges called Caitlin's house to talk to her and her family and came to her games just to see her play. She received scholarship offers from Iowa, Notre Dame, Iowa State, Texas, Oregon, and Oregon State. Caitlin had a decision to make. She was torn between her top two choices: the Notre Dame Fighting Irish and the Iowa Hawkeyes. Notre Dame was a powerhouse team and the coach, Muffet McGraw, had been one of Caitlin's idols growing up. She thought of her as one of the greatest coaches of all time. In fact, Caitlin verbally committed to going to Notre Dame. Her family was thrilled. But the closer she got to signing the official contract, something wasn't sitting quite right with her. She told ESPN, "I felt in my heart like I had to be [in Iowa]. Something was really pulling me here."

What Is the NCAA?

The National Collegiate Athletic Association (NCAA) is an organization dedicated to the well-being and lifelong success of college athletes. It was founded in 1906 to oversee college athletics and enforce the rules of play and eligibility criteria. The NCAA conducts nearly 90 national championships in sports such as basketball, football, baseball, soccer, ice hockey, and lacrosse. In 1973, the NCAA formed three different divisions (I, II, and III), and each college determines its division. Each division has unique rules about recruiting and scholarships.

IRISH
— VS —
HAWKEYES

For one thing, she wanted to stay close to home. If she went to Iowa, she could watch her little brother's basketball games and track meets and occasionally have dinner with her family. Also, Iowa had an up-tempo offense that appealed to her and an incredible crowd cheering them on. And Caitlin loved a good challenge. Iowa's head coach at the time, Lisa Bluder, had made it clear to Caitlin that she had one goal in mind: she wanted the Hawkeyes to make it to the Final Four, when the four best teams in the NCAA's Division I compete for the championship title—something Iowa had only done once before, more than 25 years earlier. Coach Bluder told Caitlin that she could help the team get there, and "I was, like, I can't pass this up," Caitlin said.

She had to listen to her heart, even though it would be a tough conversation to have with her parents and the coaches. Before she made the call to the legendary Muffet McGraw, she sat on her bed, in a sweat. How was she going to get through this? "She is an intimidating individual," Caitlin said of Coach McGraw. But when she explained her choice and why she'd made it, Coach McGraw understood. "She kinda knew. She was great," Caitlin said. Then, she called Iowa coach, Lisa Bluder, to let her know that she'd be coming there. Coach Bluder was beyond excited.

Caitlin could picture herself playing in front of fans in the Carver-Hawkeye Arena in Iowa City. She'd been to games there before with her family. The crowd was always wild, dressed in the Hawkeyes' black and gold, and the sound of their cheers reverberated in your chest. Caitlin was pumped to experience this for the first time as a Hawkeye. "If anybody watched me in high school, they know that I live

for a packed gym . . . and honestly that's one of the reasons I came to Iowa, because the support of the women's basketball team is so good," she told the *Des Moines Register*. "I just thrive off of crazy crowds."

But the start of her freshman season wasn't going to be like that. When Caitlin took to the court for her very first NCAA game, she wound up playing in front of an empty arena.

You see, this was the fall of 2020, during the height of the COVID-19 pandemic, before the vaccine was available to everyone. It was important that everyone stayed safe—avoiding large crowds helped prevent sickness. The NCAA put strict rules in place in order for teams to play at all.

A STELLAR
DEBUT

t was **November 25, 2020,** and Caitlin stepped out onto the court with her team wearing her jersey, a white shirt with black trim. On the back were her name and her new number: Clark—22. She'd be playing for the very first time as an Iowa Hawkeye in the Big Ten Conference, against in-state rival, the University of Northern Iowa. The few guests who were allowed to be there were spread out in the arena, sitting at least 6 feet (1.8 m) apart and wearing masks.

WHY NUMBER 22?

Caitlin Clark reveals the answer: "Honestly I'm not a very creative person; I was born on January 22, so it's what I went with when I was about five years old."

Caitlin could hear her heart beating in her ears. She closed her eyes and took a deep breath, and then opened them again. She felt confident. She was ready to begin.

With no crowd making noise, you could hear every sound the players made: their sneakers squeaking on the gym floor as they ran, the sound of the basketball hitting the backboard and swishing through the net, and the grunts and breaths as the players hustled around the court. It was not what she had expected, but Caitlin rose to the occasion and had an incredible debut game. She scored an impressive 27 points, caught 8 rebounds, and passed 4 assists. She made 58 percent of the shots she took. The Hawkeyes beat the Panthers 96–81.

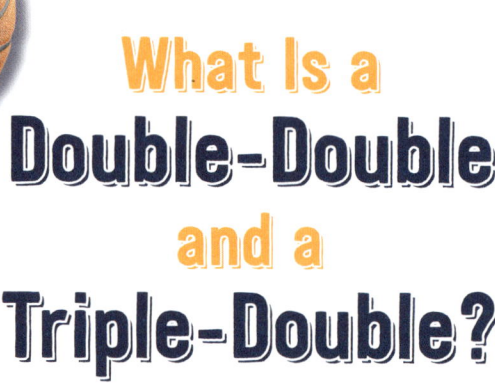

What Is a
Double-Double
and a
Triple-Double?

A basketball player records a double-double when they reach double digits (10 or more) in two of the five main statistical categories: points, rebounds, assists, blocks, and steals. A player achieves a triple-double when they have double digits in three of these categories.

Her talented teammates helped to bring in the win, including Monika Czinano with 19 points, McKenna Warnock with a double-double (14 points, 13 rebounds), and Gabbie Marshall with 11 points, including 3 three-point shots. Caitlin wasn't shocked by the outcome. "I set my goals pretty high," she told reporters.

Throughout her freshman season, Caitlin earned incredibly impressive stats. She started all 30 games for the team and led her team in scoring. But it was bigger than that: she was also the top scoring women's college basketball player that year in NCAA Division I—meaning she scored more points than anyone else from the more than 360 colleges that are part of the division! She was the first freshman player to ever do this and averaged 26.6 points per game, shooting 47.2 percent from the field. She also ranked second overall in the division for assists with 7.1 assists per game, just two of the many records she set in her rookie season.

But no matter how many accolades she received, Caitlin still wanted to do more. She had a clear goal she'd set out to help her team achieve: making it to the Final Four. The Hawkeyes made it far her freshman year. They won 20 games and lost 10, and were eliminated by UConn in the Sweet 16 round of the NCAA tournament. That wasn't good enough for Caitlin.

Caitlin was also always looking to better herself, understanding that she could never stop learning in order to be the best she could be. She worked hard and got stronger, both physically and mentally, to come into her own as a player. Standing 6 feet tall,

CRUSHING IT

In her freshman year of college, Caitlin Clark won an impressive number of awards. She was the unanimous selection for Big Ten Freshman of the Year, a basketball award given to the Big Ten Conference's most outstanding freshman player. She won the Dawn Staley Award as the best guard in the country. She shared the Tamika Catchings Award and the WBCA (Women's Basketball Coaches Association) Freshman of the Year honor with the talented UConn guard Paige Bueckers. She was also named a first-team All-American by the US Basketball Writers Association and second-team All-American by the Associated Press.

she was taller than the average point guard in the NCAA, but she was physically smaller than many of the other players in the league. She knew that she would need to focus her training in the weight room as well as on the court, getting stronger and building muscle to play with even more power and beat her opponents.

She gave her all in the gym in practice sessions, working on conditioning to increase her endurance and speed, and practicing her shots in the gym over and over again. It was hard work, but there was no place Caitlin would rather be.

6'2"

5'8"

Great
HEIGHTS

The standard height for NCAA Women's Division I players is around 5 feet, 8 inches to 6 feet, 2 inches, depending on which position they play. The players who are closest to the basket are generally the tallest so that they can catch rebounds. Point guards are often slightly shorter, averaging 5 feet, 8 inches, for both NCAA and WNBA. Caitlin Clark is 6 feet tall, giving her a slight advantage over her opponents.

Practice Makes
PERFECT

Want to practice the way Caitlin Clark does? Her private shooting sessions usually last just over one hour and consist of the following:

- **5 to 8 minutes** taking stationary shots close to the basket, working on form, and then gradually taking a step back and adding your guide hand.

- **A 300-shot routine,** which consists of 100 free throws taken behind the foul line with a goal of making 90.

- **100 mid-range jumpers** with a goal of hitting 80. This shot is taken from between the three-point line and the key or rectangle around the basket, and you jump off the ground and quickly release the ball.

- **100 three-pointers** with a goal of making 70.

- **Off-the-dribble combination shooting,** taking shots on the move.

- **Work on ball-handling** and defensive slide drills between shooting sets.

[70/100]

THREE-POINTERS

[80/100]

JUMPERS

SCHOLAR ATHLETE

In addition to maintaining a rigorous practice schedule, Caitlin also made sure to keep up with her studies. She had decided to major in marketing and minor in communications. These subjects would help her to one day run her own nonprofit and apply her education to her own basketball brand. She could see herself pursuing sports management or team ownership one day. An honors student, she managed to maintain a 3.64 GPA throughout college, studying just as hard as she played. It wasn't always easy to stay balanced, though.

Caitlin knew, in order to say grounded, centered, and focused, that she had to lean on the people who knew her best. Her family was always there to support her, including her parents, Brent and Anne; her paternal grandmother, Carole Clark; her maternal grandfather, Bob Nizzi; and her brothers, Blake and Colin.

Her brothers were her biggest supporters. Sometimes, she playfully referred to them as "haters," because they wouldn't let it slide if she missed a shot or messed up in a game. They were often the first ones to "text and say something funny," giving

March Madness is the nickname for the NCAA's Division I basketball tournament. The tournament begins in mid-March and continues until the beginning of April. Sixty-eight teams are chosen to compete, with 32 entered automatically and the rest selected by a committee, based on team performance throughout the regular season. The committee also "seeds"–or ranks–the teams and decides where to "plant" them in the tournament. The rankings are announced on **Selection Sunday**.

The number of teams gets halved, from 64 in the first round to 32 in the second round. The final few rounds of the competition include the **Sweet 16**, **Elite Eight**, and **Final Four**. The last two teams left standing then compete in the **National Championship**.

her a hard time—in a loving way, of course. And she was there to playfully tease them and cheer them on, too, as both her brothers went on to achieve athletic excellence themselves. Her older brother Blake played football at Iowa State University and her younger brother Colin ran track and played basketball in high school. Caitlin and Blake would go back to their old high school to cheer on their little brother whenever they could.

Caitlin did an incredible job balancing the pressures that came with schoolwork and her intense practice schedule, excelling at all she put her mind to. But one of her biggest struggles was managing her emotions when things weren't going her

way. If Caitlin didn't perform her best, she was her own toughest critic. She was just as hard on the other players when she felt they also weren't putting in as much effort as they could or not taking the game seriously enough. Sometimes, the high expectations she carried for herself and everyone else felt like a heavy load—and sometimes, she felt a little bit lonely, as if she were carrying it all by herself.

Caitlin still had the competitive fire that had driven her since she was a kid, and she was still learning how to express it in healthy ways. She still wore all her feelings

THERE ARE MANY WAYS

to be a team player, whether you can be loud or prefer to be quiet. Lift up your teammates and friends to help them succeed. Consider how other people do things and be flexible about trying it their way.

and emotions on the outside. She lost her temper in practice and in games when she or her teammates weren't performing well. She would throw her hands up in the air and stomp off the court or refuse to pass teammates the ball if she didn't think they'd be able to deliver.

Caitlin's teammates could feel her disappointment and frustration. On the flip side, they also felt pride when she complimented them or did rely on them in the game. Caitlin was not afraid to be herself and speak her mind. If she didn't like what you were doing, she'd let you know, but if she thought you did a great job, you'd know that too. It wasn't personal. It was basketball.

Caitlin was slowly learning she didn't have to carry her extraordinarily high expectations alone. She had a team who was ready and willing to support her. If they were going to reach their goals, they needed to rely on each other and work together. It would take time for Caitlin and the other players to trust one another and to learn how to work together as a team.

Taking Home the GOLD

In August 2021, Caitlin Clark competed with the US junior national team at the 2021 FIBA Under-19 Women's Basketball World Cup in Debrecen, Hungary. This was an international tournament organized by FIBA (the International Basketball Federation) for women's youth national teams, open to players aged 19 and younger, and Caitlin led the United States to the gold medal! With 14.3 points, 5.6 assists, and 5.3 rebounds per game, Caitlin was named Most Valuable Player and made the All-Tournament team. It was also the first time she played alongside some of the women she would later compete against in some of her biggest moments.

CHAPTER

STAR ON
THE RISE

THE
SCRIMMAGE

———

In 2021, the fall of her sophomore season, things started to click for Caitlin and the Iowa Hawkeyes. During a preseason scrimmage, Caitlin's side was losing with four minutes left. Something came over Caitlin that would set the tone for her season, and she just started launching the ball at the net. She hit a two-pointer, then a three-pointer, then another three. Swish. Swish. Swish. For some of the shots, she was off balance, one leg in the air. But they kept going in the basket. She hit five three-pointers in a row. The coaches and other players watched her in complete awe. They knew she had incredible talent, but they didn't know she could do that.

A little later in the season, the same force came over her in a game against Michigan. That season, the crowds were a little bit larger than they had been the previous year, but were still not back to the pre-COVID size. Still, it felt good to feel the pulse and energy of a crowd again.

Late in the third quarter, Iowa was down by 25 points. Caitlin started draining three-pointers—some fired from far away, near the half-court line where the **team logo** was painted. She hit four in a row, bringing the Hawkeyes within 5 points of Michigan. She scored a total of 46 points that game, the most points she'd ever scored in a single college game. Twenty-five of those points, she landed in the fourth quarter. She pumped her fists and lifted her arms to the crowd. The fans went wild.

That day, the Hawkeyes didn't pull off the win, losing 98–90, but they still had something to feel good about. Caitlin had stunned her teammates. With a talent like that, they had the sense that they'd be bringing in more wins very soon.

LOGO 3

The fact that Caitlin could consistently drain these deep three-pointers wasn't accidental, and it wasn't magic. She had put in years and years of tireless practice and hard work to be able to shoot the ball like that. She had practiced for days on end in the driveway. She had studied players like Steph Curry and Maya Moore on TV. She had been playing basketball from the time she could walk, her dad standing beside her as she set up for the shot, coaching her on how to keep her hips square and stay focused on the target. Caitlin had put in the hard work to perfect her winning shot, and suddenly, it was all coming together. She had found her rhythm.

Caitlin honed her craft by doing reps in the gym alone. She spent time in the weight room, too, strengthening and conditioning her body. The power of the shot came from her legs. She had done the work behind the scenes, and it was paying off.

STAYING STRONG

A powerful and accurate shot comes from a strong body, particularly, as Caitlin says, strong legs. How does Caitlin build muscle and strengthen her legs? In addition to her rigorous shooting practice, she does sprints, squats, jumps, dead lifts, lunges, single-leg work, and ankle stability exercises.

Once Coach Bluder saw just how accurately and consistently Caitlin could deliver three-point shots, she encouraged her to keep at it. Her team started to rely on her for this. Opponents had a hard time defending her, especially when she was on a roll. She could take a shot from almost anywhere on the court—nowhere was safe.

**25' to 30'
(7.6 to 9.1 m)**

**22' 1¾"
(6.8 m)**

LONG SHOTS

According to NCAA rules, the three-point line on college basketball courts is 22 feet, 1¾ inches (6.8 m) from the basket's rim. Caitlin's three-point shots were often launched from even farther away, 25 to 30 feet (7.6 to 9.1 m) from the basket. Caitlin was better at shooting these long balls than just about anyone. While the NCAA average for shots from this distance was about 30 percent, almost 40 percent of Caitlin's logo shots went in.

ASSISTS

Not only was Caitlin a major threat when it came to scoring, she was a leader in assists as well. She could throw a pinpoint pass, a no-look pass to a player on her right, or a behind-the-back pass to someone on her left. She had incredible court vision, or an awareness of where everyone was around her, and an instinct to pass the ball to whoever was in the best position to score. She could react quickly to the changing dynamics of the game. She and her teammates were learning how to effectively make plays together. When Caitlin saw an opportunity to pass the ball and get an assist, her teammates also needed to be sure to be there to receive it.

Caitlin's playmaking showed intelligence and creativity on the court, which also made her fun to watch. Her former high school coach at Dowling, Kristin Meyer, knew Caitlin would be great in college, but had no idea just how great. "Her court vision. Her understanding. I haven't seen a higher IQ," Coach Meyer said in an interview. "It's an art. She can make it look effortless."

Sharing Is Caring

Scoring points is obviously crucial, but basketball is not a solo sport. Knowing when to pass the ball makes you a good team player. When you can set someone else up to score, you are showing that you are there to support your teammates and make sure everyone gets a chance to shine.

PASSES

There are generally two broad categories for basketball passes: air passes that reach another player without touching the floor and bounce passes that hit the floor before reaching your teammate. Within those categories, there are different ways to send the ball across the court. These are a few basic passes:

- **Chest Pass:** This is a common way to pass the ball, by throwing it from chest level to a teammate, especially when the player has a clear line of sight. This pass is a quick and accurate way to send the ball to a teammate. It can also be called a push pass.

- **Bounce Pass:** The bounce pass, or bouncing the ball to the floor to an open teammate, is another common way to handle the ball. It can be used to get the ball around a defender's legs and is effective when a player is cutting back to the basket and gets in position to catch the ball.

- **Overhead Pass:** Here, the player passes the ball over a defender's head. It's most effective when the player you're passing to is farther down the court. This can also be called a skip pass.

These passes are more advanced:

- **Alley-Oop Pass:** A player throws the ball above the rim of the basket to a teammate who jumps up high to dunk the ball. Alley-oop or lob passes are very difficult to execute but make for a good show!

- **No-Look Pass:** A player passes to a teammate without looking at them. The ball handler needs to have complete vision of the court in order to know, without looking directly, when teammates are in good position to receive the ball. It's a great way to fake out a defender.

- **Behind-the-Back Pass:** This is when a player wraps the ball around their back for a teammate to grab and is great for getting around a defender. This pass works best for connecting with an open teammate on the opposite side of the player's dominant dribbling hand.

- **Hook Pass:** Also known as the skyhook pass or the Kareem Abdul-Jabbar pass, for this pass, the ball handler passes the ball with a hook-like motion off one hand. This is an effective way to get around a close defender—especially their outstretched arms.

- **Off-the-Dribble Pass:** When a player uses a dribble pass, they dribble the ball and then immediately throw it to an open teammate. This is often a one-handed pass that happens while dribbling.

- **Diagonal Pass:** With anticipation and accuracy, a player throws the ball diagonally to a teammate who might not be in their initial line of sight.

CREIGHTON UPSET

The Hawkeyes were having a great season, and Caitlin was more than ready to face the goal she'd set out to achieve: making it to the Final Four. First, the team would have to make it back to the Sweet 16 like they had in Caitlin's freshman year.

Iowa fans crammed into the Carver-Hawkeye Arena, hoping to see a history-making game. Iowa was ranked as the number two seed, and their opponent, the Creighton Bluejays, was number 10. People were expecting the higher-ranked Iowa to pull out the win and move to the next round.

The Bluejays knew that if they wanted any chance of winning, they would have to find a way to stop Caitlin Clark. To keep Caitlin from scoring, the Bluejays planned

CRUSHING IT

Caitlin started smashing records in her sophomore season. She broke the Carver-Hawkeye Arena women's single-game scoring record when she scored those 46 points in the game against Michigan. In a home game against Evansville, she sank a deep three-pointer and surpassed Kelsey Mitchell (a top scoring player on Ohio State who would later become Caitlin's teammate on the Fever) as the fastest Big Ten player to reach 1,000 career points. In a 93–83 victory game against Nebraska, she recorded a triple-double for the fourth time in her career with 31 points, 10 rebounds, and 10 assists in the game.

She was chosen as a first-team unanimous All-American. She also became the first women's player to be a leader in points and assists in a single season. She became the first Division I player (of both men's and women's teams) to record consecutive triple-doubles with at least 30 points and the first women's player in Big Ten history with consecutive triple-doubles.

to rotate their defenders on her, stifling her. A key part of this plan was Creighton guard Lauren Jensen, who had transferred from Iowa to Creighton just that season. Lauren was playing on what used to be her home court against the team she'd only recently left.

This tactic worked in the Bluejays' favor. Caitlin had a rare off-game, scoring only 15 points, her lowest total of the season. She also had only 11 assists, another record low. Her teammates were also off, with baskets hitting the rim and bouncing

off, a number of sloppy turnovers, and missed rebounds. Lauren Jensen, on the other hand, dominated on the court, scoring 9 of the last 10 points for the Bluejays.

Caitlin had a hard time keeping her frustration to herself. She threw her hands in the air when a ref didn't call an opponent's foul. After all, she was the same person who had accidentally pushed her brother into a wall when she had lost a NERF game, and the same kid who would cry when she lost in a board game. "I think I'm an emotional player no matter the situation, good or bad," she said in a press conference. "I think that's how I'm going to play really if we're winning, we're losing, I'm playing good, I'm playing bad."

At the end of the fourth quarter, with only 12 seconds remaining, the score was 62–60 with Iowa in the lead. Then Lauren Jensen nailed a three-pointer that pushed Creighton into the lead. Iowa needed just one more basket to take it back. Caitlin received a pass and drove the ball to the left side of the lane. She put the ball up and it hit the glass, but it didn't land. Teammate Monika Czinano's last hook shot seemed to hang on the rim, everyone on the edge of their seats, but the ball didn't go in. After one more point on a foul shot, Creighton won the game 64–62. For the first time in the Bluejays' history, they were advancing to the Sweet 16.

The Hawkeyes, on the other hand, were done for the season. They felt like they had been punched in the gut. They hadn't expected to lose so early in the tournament. Afterward, they sat in the locker room with their heads in their hands.

Caitlin was crushed. This loss hit her particularly hard. She felt as if she hadn't pulled her weight and was disappointed in her performance.

"I just feel bad for the fans because they've given us so much over these past two weeks," Caitlin said in a postgame press conference. "I think there's a lot of exciting basketball ahead for this group, but obviously the feeling of letting them down, letting the coaches down, our teammates down, it stinks right now, but I think overall just more fuel for us going into next year."

The Hawkeyes didn't wallow for long. Very quickly, they pulled each other back up and brushed themselves off. The season had come to an abrupt end, but they had the summer to train. Next year, they would come back bigger and better. And for Caitlin, that feeling of being punched in the gut was a sensation she never wanted to experience again. She reminded herself of that feeling whenever she was dragging in practice. Her older brother Blake wouldn't let her forget it either. He would send a photo of the scoreboard to his sister at random moments to get her going: *Creighton 64, Iowa 62.* "She eats that stuff up," Blake told ESPN.

This loss stoked Caitlin's competitive fire more than ever before. "From your greatest failures can come your greatest successes," she told herself.

HISTORIC UPSET

The biggest upset for women's college basketball occurred in 1998, when Harvard, No. 16 seed, defeated the No. 1 seed, Stanford, 71–67. More than 25 years later, this remains the greatest upset in NCAA women's tournament history.

CHAPTER

THE CAITLIN CLARK EFFECT

JUNIOR YEAR

n the fall of 2022, Caitlin Clark began her junior year at Iowa. Over the previous two years, she'd honed her craft and proven herself to be a strong player, all while doing well in her studies. She had also experienced what it felt like to lose and not to perform to the best of her abilities, and she had learned to pick herself back up from that disappointment.

Unlike those previous years, the arena would be full in late 2022. Some of the COVID restrictions had been lifted and more and more people were coming out to watch sports. The sound of the crowd excited Caitlin and pumped her up to get out there and play.

So many fans were there to see Caitlin drain logo shots, pinpoint open

Can Women Trash-Talk?

Many women athletes face harsh judgment when they are competitive on the court. Caitlin Clark has received criticism for showing intense emotions, questioning the referees, and pushing back against opponents. Other players, such as Stanford's Cameron Brink and LSU's Angel Reese, have also experienced such backlash. The question is: Do men receive the same kind of criticism? Caitlin has said that women should be able to trash-talk opponents just as men do. "Men have always had trash talk," she said. "You should be able to play with that emotion . . . that's how every girl should continue to play."

players, and drive past defenders. They were also there to see her showmanship and swagger. After a good shot, she'd gesture toward the crowd with her arms outstretched, with a proud smile on her face. She also showed her fiery side, letting the refs know if she didn't like a call, showing frustration in her body language when her team was down. She would trash-talk the other players, too, if they fouled her or got in her way. She was still that scrappy five-year-old girl who refused to be bullied by a boy twice her size. And the crowd loved it.

"People need to start understanding that women can play with that same passion and competitive spirit that men have played with for years," Caitlin told *Iowa Everywhere*. "That's what's attracting people to our game—when women are fiery, when they're competitive, when they're feisty, when they're encouraging their teammates."

MEDIA ATTENTION

—

A whirlwind of excitement was starting to gather around women's college basketball at this time, with Caitlin Clark at the epicenter. TV cameras were always on her, watching her every reaction, expression, and move on the court. Suddenly, the NCAA women's basketball teams were playing in front of sold-out arenas. There was an enormous boost in ticket sales.

Kids lined up before and after games hoping for an autograph or a chance to say hello, just as Caitlin had done for her favorite players when she was a kid. She never forgot how it felt when her role model, Maya Moore, had smiled and said hi to her. Something as simple as giving a kid a high five or signing the back of their shirt could brighten their day. It meant everything to Caitlin to see the joy in their faces.

OMG, I'M... THE SHOE GIRL

A New York teen went viral after getting an autograph from Caitlin Clark. Makaya McCann was a 15-year-old high school basketball player with high hopes of getting recruited to a place like Iowa. At first, Makaya didn't understand "all the hype" around Caitlin—but that quickly changed the second she saw her play in person. Suddenly, she was a superfan.

She was going to a big game to see Iowa play LSU. She figured there was "no way" she could get Caitlin's autograph with the swarms of people lined up, but she took her chances. Makaya waited until after the game and then took off one of her Nike Blazer high-tops, holding it out for over 40 minutes. "I was, like, 'I *need* Caitlin to sign my shoe,'" she said.

Caitlin was moving down the line of kids with her pen in hand, signing autographs on posters, basketballs, and the backs of kids' number 22 jerseys.

Finally, Caitlin reached Makaya and signed her shoe. Makaya's wide-eyed, open-mouthed expression was priceless. "Oh my god!" Makaya yelled. The joyful clip went viral and played on several news stations. Mayaka called in to one of the stations and said, "I'm the shoe girl!" She was then interviewed about the experience on TV.

Hawkeyes' fans started sending Makaya messages of support, letting her know they hoped they could cheer for her as a Hawkeye one day. She keeps the signed sneaker in a glass box and vows to never wear it again.

SPONSORSHIP

The newfound popularity of women's basketball brought more opportunities for the players.

In 2021, the NCAA changed its rules and allowed college athletes to earn money for their "name, image, and likeness" (NIL). Through these NIL deals, individual players were able to secure sponsorship deals with companies.

One of Caitlin's very first partnerships was with a grocery store in her area called Hy-Vee. They produced a cereal called Caitlin's Crunch Time with a picture of her on the box. A portion of the proceeds went to the Caitlin Clark Foundation, a nonprofit that aims to "uplift and improve the lives of youth and their communities through education, nutrition, and sport."

As her national profile grew, Caitlin went on to partner with iconic brands like Nike, Gatorade, Buick, and State Farm. At Nike, she joined a roster of legendary athletes who had been sponsored by the brand, including Michael Jordan, Serena Williams, and Megan Rapinoe. In one ad, she is shown holding a basketball, standing in front of a fallen hoop, bricks scattered on the floor around her. "Before you build something new, you have to break some ground," she said.

In a Gatorade reel, clips of Caitlin as a kid playing basketball with her team play, then cut to her shooting the basketball as a pro. "I was once that little Iowa girl who was inspired to dream big, real big," she said. "And that dream was more than women's basketball. It was possibility that I turned into reality. I'm still that girl from Iowa. But now, it's my turn to inspire. If I can drop 40, you can drop 50. If we can draw 56,000 fans, you can draw 57. If I can sign with Gatorade, you can too."

Name, Image, and
Likeness

The NCAA once enforced strict laws that required college athletes to remain pure amateurs, with no way to earn money without risking their eligibility. That changed after a Supreme Court ruling in 2021, which declared that student-athletes were permitted to earn money for their "name, image, and likeness" (NIL). They could now get paid by brands like Nike or Gatorade when their name, picture, or signature moves appeared in commercials and magazines or on social media. NIL deals have made it possible for athletes to profit from their sport and talent, market themselves, and build a public profile.

THE CAITLIN CLARK
EFFECT

People started coming out in droves to watch one of the highest scorers in women's NCAA history, and Caitlin Clark suddenly became a household name. Everyone seemed to know about her, everyone was talking about her, and everyone wanted to watch her play. Viewership of the women's game soared both on TV and in person. Fans packed into stadiums like never before. Something incredible was happening here. Caitlin was becoming a cultural phenomenon. The media started talking about "The Caitlin Clark Effect," describing the effect she was having not only on the game, but popular culture as well. The attention Caitlin was drawing was also beginning to change the atmosphere around the game.

Later in the 2022–2023 season, there would be an average of 9.9 *million* TV viewers of the NCAA Division I Women's Basketball tournament, more than double

9,900,000

Sedona Prince
and Gender Equality

Sedona Prince, who played college basketball for Texas, Oregon, and Texas Christian University, made headlines in 2021 with a 38-second viral TikTok video. In it, she showed the difference between the weight rooms for the men's and women's basketball teams at Oregon. While the men had access to an entire weight room decked out with a wide array of equipment, the women's "room" was a much smaller space with just one small stack of dumbbells.

Sedona talked more about gender inequalities in the sport, using these differences as a starting point. While women athletes were finally allowed to make money from sponsorships, men were still being given better opportunities.

After her video went viral, there was an outcry on social media. In response, the NCAA hired a law firm to review the situation, and they ultimately found a lot of inequities between men's and women's teams. The NCAA provided the men's teams with better quality food, better advertising, and better practice facilities.

Since then, the NCAA has been working toward equality. Now, they are providing women with the same kinds of swag bags the men receive, with branded T-shirts, hats, towels, and other gifts. They are spending millions more than years before on the women's tournament. They have expanded the women's tournament from 64 to 68 teams, the same number of teams in the men's tournament, and, in 2022, they started branding the women's tournament as "March Madness," just like the men's tournament.

There's still a long road to equality, but Sedona Prince's willingness to speak up helped to get things moving in the right direction.

the viewership of the year before. Attendance at the stadiums would also set new records, with 19,482 fans packed into the arena to watch the championship game in 2023. The Women's March Madness games that year hit an all-time attendance record with 357,542 fans.

In the past, women's basketball had not received the same kind of attention as men's basketball, at both the college and professional levels. Men's basketball in general brought in a lot more fans and viewers.

While the women's game has made a lot of progress, it still lags far behind the men's league in terms of pay. In 2023, the highest-paid WNBA player made a salary of $242,000, while the lowest salary in the NBA was over a million dollars. In 2024, the highest-paid NBA player made a salary of $55 million dollars, while the highest-paid WNBA player made a salary of $338,000. The men's professional teams also got to travel to games in style on private charter flights, while women's teams took commercial flights.

Title IX

Caitlin's rise to popularity was impacting women's basketball for the better, and it was also fulfilling the promise of Title IX. Title IX is a civil rights law that was passed in 1972, making sure that girls have the same rights as boys in educational settings. When it comes to athletics, girls have not historically had the same opportunities as boys. Universities would spend more money on boys' sports. Because of this, locker rooms, equipment, and training programs were not as good for the girls' teams. There is still a very long way to go, but Caitlin's popularity, sponsorship deals, and record-breaking career were all examples of the huge strides made in women's athletics and the fight for gender equality.

As women's basketball has gained popularity, more and more tickets have been sold, meaning more money for the athletic departments of their colleges. The hope is that this money will inspire schools to provide better resources for their women's teams, like improved training programs and locker rooms. This investment should inspire more young women athletes, elevating the sport even higher.

The Caitlin Clark Effect was putting women's basketball in the spotlight and young girls across the country were watching. *If Caitlin can do this, I can too.*

IT TAKES A
TEAM

Caitlin felt grateful for the hype, the attention, and the recognition, but she never lost sight of how important her team was to her. This was not a one-person show. She had incredible athletes around her like Hawkeyes forward McKenna Warnock, a consistent and versatile player, and someone that Caitlin called, "a calming presence on the team." There was also Gabbie Marshall, a great shooter and a defensive stopper who could steal the ball in clutch moments. Caitlin praised her defensive skills, telling the *Daily Iowan*, "She takes the challenge of guarding the best player every single game." Kate Martin, a Hawkeyes guard who was commonly referred to as the "glue" holding the team together, was "probably the best leader I've ever been around in my entire life," Caitlin said. "She is somebody you want on your team no matter what sport it is, male or female." And Monika Czinano, Hawkeyes center, was a pillar of strength who shot a remarkable 67 percent from the field over the course of her entire career.

Caitlin and Monika formed an incredible bond and came to rely on each other on and off the court. They celebrated happy moments together, and they also offered each other a shoulder to cry on more than once after a disappointing game. Coach Bluder described Clark and Czinano as one of the best point guard and center duos in the nation.

THE LAW FIRM

Caitlin Clark and Monika Czinano were nicknamed "The Law Firm of Clark and Czinano," or "The Law Firm," earning a reputation as the best post-guard combo in the country.

PATH TO
FINAL FOUR

The Hawkeyes were having an incredible season, but they still kept the loss to Creighton in the back of their minds at all times as motivation. This year, they would not allow an upset like that to happen again.

This would be the last season for two incredible starters on the team. Monika Czinano would be leaving Iowa to play in a European pro league the following year, and McKenna Warnock was graduating. The Hawkeyes had to capitalize on the opportunity to use two of their best players and get to work.

After blowing out Southeastern Louisiana by a score of 95–43 in the first round, Iowa beat Georgia 74–66 in the second round. So far, so good—they were off to Seattle.

At the start of the Sweet 16, the Hawkeyes had an easy win against Colorado. Caitlin scored 31 points that game.

Now it was time for the Elite Eight game against Louisville. Caitlin walked onto the court with a cool calm about her. Somehow, she didn't feel nervous at all. She was focused, in the zone. This was the biggest game of her life up until this point, and she had the sense that it was going to be a good one.

After draining her sixth three-pointer, Caitlin made a "you can't see me" hand motion, waving her hand in front of her face to show that she's unstoppable. This move was popularized by WWE wrestler John Cena along with the catchphrase, "You can't see me"—as in, "I'm so fast, I'm invisible." Cena tweeted a response, singing

CRUSHING IT

Once again, Caitlin was breaking records left and right. In her junior year, she was named Big Ten preseason Player of the Year and became a Big Ten career leader in triple-doubles. She tied with two-time WNBA MVP Elena Delle Donne to become the fastest Division I women's player to reach 2,000 career points. She was the unanimous Big Ten Player of the Year and was named first-team All-Big Ten. She was the first player in men's or women's NCAA tournament history to record a 30- or 40-point triple-double, first Division I player to record at least 900 points and 300 assists in a single season, and first player in NCAA tournament history with consecutive 40-point games. She won Best Female College Athlete ESPY Award, the Honda Cup, the James E. Sullivan Award, and Big Ten Female Athlete of the Year—and that's only the start!

Caitlin's praises: "Even if they could see you . . . they couldn't guard you! Congrats on the historic performance @CaitlinClark22 . . . "

And a historic performance it was. In this game, Caitlin became the very first player in either women's or men's NCAA tournament history to reach a 40-point triple-double. She scored 41 points and had 12 assists and 10 rebounds.

The score was 48–47 before halftime, with the Hawkeyes in the lead. After halftime, the Hawkeyes scored 11 points in a row. The crowd of nearly 12,000 rose to their feet. The Hawkeyes finished the game with a 97–83 win over Louisville. Iowa had done it. They were headed to the Final Four!

Caitlin hugged **Coach Bluder**, celebrating the achievement of the goal they'd shared. The team ran to each other, jumping up and embracing each other, as confetti fell from the ceiling. Caitlin held the regional trophy over her head, parading around the court as the fans cheered.

Caitlin said in a post-game interview, "When I came here, I said I wanted to take this program to the Final Four, and all you've got to do is dream. And all you've got to do is believe and work your butt off to get there. That's what I did, and that's what our girls did and that's what our coaches did and we're going to Dallas, baby."

FINAL FOUR
CHAPIONSHIP

There were still more games to go, though, before they could make it to the championship. Caitlin again felt calm and almost peaceful as she walked out onto the court to battle the South Carolina Gamecocks. She knew she had put in the hard work and now it was just time to get out there and play her best. South Carolina was a great team, undefeated during the regular season and the number one seed in the tournament. Beating them would not be an easy feat. But the Hawkeyes played an incredible game. Caitlin, once again, scored 41 points in this game, becoming the sixth player ever to score over 1,000 points in a season. And with an incredible performance, Iowa won again, in a victory of 77–73!

The Hawkeyes were off to the championship game against the LSU Tigers. LSU was a strong team with powerhouse players like Angel Reese, who had won the All-Southeastern-Conference Player of the Year award and would be named Most Outstanding Player of the Final Four. LSU's strategy was to prevent Caitlin's

teammates Monika Czinano and McKenna Warnock from scoring, in the hopes that Caitlin's baskets wouldn't be enough on their own.

Their strategy worked. While Caitlin had a historic performance, breaking the all-time NCAA tournament scoring record and scoring the most three-pointers in an NCAA Championship game, it just wasn't enough. Iowa lost 102–85.

In the locker room, the Hawkeyes didn't just cry, they "bawled," Caitlin told ESPN. Caitlin and her friend Kate Martin formed a

group hug with their teammates McKenna Warnock and **Monika Czinano**, who had just played the final game of their NCAA careers. These women had been through so much together; they had formed a bond like family.

In a post-game press conference, Caitlin expressed her intense disappointment, but also pride in all they'd accomplished. "I want my legacy to be the impact that I have on young kids and the people in the state of Iowa," she said through tears. "I hope I brought them a lot of joy this season. I hope this team brought them a lot of joy. I understand we came up one win short, but I think we have a lot to be proud of and a lot to celebrate. I was just that young girl, so all you have to do is dream, and you can be in moments like this."

DOUBLE
STANDARD

After the winner was named, the media was still talking about the game, but not just because of the teams' performances.

In the fourth quarter, when it seemed clear that LSU was about to win, **Angel Reese** had made a hand gesture to Caitlin that caused a media frenzy. She waved her hand in front of her face, in the same "you can't see me" move Caitlin had flashed in a previous game, then pointed at her ring finger, as if to say, "I'm the one getting the championship ring."

The gesture went viral. Many people criticized Angel, some commentators even referring to her as "classless" and calling the gesture unsportsmanlike. But others, including professional athletes, came to Angel's defense, noting the racist double standard. Two games earlier, Caitlin had made the exact same gesture to one of her opponents. The difference was that Caitlin is white and Angel is Black.

This moment brought up an important discussion about race. There was a debate about how the media and the public have not always given Black women's basketball players the same treatment, respect, or attention that white players received. No one seemed to be disputing the fact that Caitlin Clark was one of the most talented and captivating basketball players out there. But have athletes who are Black, and who are just as talented, been treated

the same? Do Black and white players receive the same kinds of endorsement deals from iconic brands like Nike and Gatorade? Have they gotten the same kinds of airtime on TV?

Victoria Jackson, a sports historian, commented on the issue in an article on AP News. "There are basketball reasons," she said. "But also there are racial reasons for why Clark has been able to kind of break off into a completely different stratosphere from players that came before her."

Jackson went on to say that too often, Black athletes who are considered "generational talents" like Caitlin Clark "have not had that sort of gushing attention." It is important and necessary to talk about these issues to make sure that we are always working toward "equitable treatment of the athletes in the sport." Conversations like these must continue to better the sport and to ensure that everyone is treated fairly.

While the media liked to spin the relationship between Caitlin Clark and Angel Reese as a rivalry, the players themselves didn't see it that way. In fact, they had a lot of respect for one another. They were both just out there playing to win.

Caitlin immediately defended Angel Reese in an ESPN interview. "I don't think Angel should be criticized at all. I'm just one that competes, and she competed. I think everybody knew there was going to be a little trash talk in the entire tournament. It's not just me and Angel." She added, "You know, Angel is a tremendous, tremendous player. I have nothing but respect for her. I love her game—the way she rebounds the ball, scores the ball, it's absolutely incredible. I'm a big fan of her and even the entire LSU team. They played an amazing game."

After the "you can't see me" fiasco, Angel Reese made it clear that she had no animosity toward Caitlin: "Oh my gosh, I love Caitlin; we've been competing since we were in AAU [a youth basketball organization]." She told reporters, "It was always fun, always competitive. One day, hopefully, we could even be teammates. She is a great player, shooter, person, and teammate."

In fact, in just a few short years, Angel's prediction would come true, and they would have the opportunity to play together in a whole new league.

CHAPTER

THE NCAA CHAMPIONSHIP AND GOING PRO

CAITLIN'S
SENIOR YEAR

Heading into her senior year at Iowa, Caitlin was carrying a lot of weight on her shoulders. She felt how important it was to uphold the standards that she had set for herself and the expectations of everyone around her. The season before, she had helped to take the Hawkeyes to the Final Four for the first time in 30 years. Everyone was counting on her and the team to do it again.

In the meantime, she had been catapulted to a whole new level of fame. Wherever she went, there were fans sporting number 22 jerseys, calling out her name. There was a whole fan base that had been nicknamed "Clarkies," like Taylor Swift's fan base of "Swifties." She even made TV appearances, including in the "Weekend Update" segment of *Saturday Night Live*, the live comedy sketch show.

Attendance at the stadiums soared when Caitlin Clark was there to play. People traveled far and wide, lining up in the morning for an evening game, and waiting in long lines in frigid weather. Some teams had to move to different arenas to accommodate the number of seats needed, and ticket prices skyrocketed when Caitlin was on the roster. She also now had to travel with security, even just to get from the locker room to the court.

The term "#Clarkonomics" was used to describe the way that Caitlin was impacting the economics of college sports, or how much money women's basketball was beginning to bring in thanks to her popularity. The term was first coined by Deb Antonelli, a basketball analyst who gives expert commentary on the sport. Deb commented on the high ticket prices to see a game. In 2024, the cost of a ticket to see Caitlin Clark play at Ohio State was $1,475. Deb tweeted, "Unprecedented for a college women's basketball player! Don't know if in my decades in the game I've ever seen this!"

DECIDING ABOUT
THE DRAFT

In the middle of all the excitement, Caitlin had a decision to make. She had to decide if this would be her last season as an Iowa Hawkeye.

The WNBA, the world's top professional women's basketball league, would soon be holding its 2024 draft, during which teams select new players from the pool of eligible college athletes. Caitlin was eligible to enter the draft after her 22nd birthday—or she could decide to play college basketball for one more year. (The NCAA allowed any athletes who participated in winter sports in the 2020–2021 season an extra season of eligibility because their season had been cut short due to COVID-19.)

Caitlin had dreamed of being in the WNBA since she was a little kid. But she had a lot to consider. Would she be able to maintain the same level of success in the WNBA that she had in college basketball? And how could she leave the Hawkeyes behind when they were just hitting their stride and creating something beautiful together?

She went to her coaches and to her family to ask their advice, weighing the pros and cons and looking at the decision from every angle.

After careful consideration, on February 29, Caitlin announced that she would be entering the draft. While she would miss so much about college basketball, especially her teammates and her coaches, she was ready for the next challenge. At an Iowa press conference, she said, "I knew in my heart here that what we've been able to do is so special, and that it's not over yet, but I think I'm ready for the next chapter in my life, too."

Once the decision was made, it was time for her to make the most of the days she had left as a Hawkeye. That season, Iowa had a lot of highs and lows, wins and losses. It was a challenge that so many star players had graduated, including two of the women Caitlin had come to think of as sisters, Monika and McKenna. Caitlin had to adjust to playing with new teammates. But the team, once again, found their stride and Caitlin achieved a lot of personal goals too.

Heading into a matchup with Michigan on February 15, 2024, Caitlin was expected to hit a huge milestone. She was coming into the game with 3,520 career points. Eight more points and Caitlin would become the NCAA women's all-time scorer, besting Washington's Kelsey Plum's record of 3,527 points. The question was, when would she do it? The stadium was packed, ready to celebrate the moment it happened.

Caitlin quickly racked up points right off the bat, hitting a layup and a deep three-pointer.

"Number 22!" an ESPN announcer said. "From the outside! Oh, this is going to happen quick."

Now she had to score only 3 points to break Kelsey Plum's record. Gabbie Marshall recovered the ball after a turnover and passed it off to Caitlin. She dribbled down the court, stopping just past half court.

"How will she go for history?" the announcer said.

It was only 2 minutes and 12 seconds into the game. Caitlin shot a 35-foot (10 m) logo jumper that rolled off her fingertips, soared over her defender's outstretched hands and *swished* through the net—hitting the remaining three points in one stop. With these 3 points, Caitlin became the NCAA women's all-time Division I scoring leader.

The moment the ball went through the net, the packed Carver-Hawkeye Arena erupted in deafening cheers, the crowd of Iowa and Michigan fans alike getting to their feet. Caitlin pumped her arms and yelled out in celebration with the audience. Caitlin's parents and brothers were there watching in the stands, cheering and hugging each other. Though she hadn't planned on doing it, Coach Bluder called a timeout so the team could take a moment to celebrate Caitlin's achievement. Caitlin's teammates enveloped her in a hug, and then Caitlin made a point to find her coach to embrace her.

Caitlin kept smashing records after that. On March 3, 2024, she set up to take two free throws after a technical foul in a game against Ohio State, and made both shots. With those points, she beat **Pete Maravich's** record, making her the Division I scoring leader among both women *and* men.

Full CIRCLE

Caitlin has never forgotten what it felt like, as a kid, to meet her idol, basketball legend **Maya Moore**. That chance came around again years later, in March 2024. In an ESPN interview just before one of Caitlin's Iowa games against Ohio State in her senior year, Maya Moore walked around the corner to surprise her.

Caitlin screamed and brought her hands to her mouth. "Oh my gosh!" she said, giddy and flustered. "I'm fangirling so hard."

The players hugged and Caitlin thanked Maya for coming. She said, "I still feel like I'm this tall and I ran across the court and gave you a hug . . . all I ever wanted to do was meet [you]. It's the most vivid memory I have of women's basketball growing up . . . it meant so much to me."

Maya was touched and said, "Full circle moment. I remember being 10-year-old Maya, going up, hugging Cynthia Cooper or one of the legends. Just to see that we're still continuing to be connected and to be inspired by each other, to be *family*. I love the connection. . . . It is so cool to see little seeds like that of how we treat each other, of how we see each other, of how we enjoy each other and what that means."

She also mentioned how proud she was of Caitlin. "Now she's grown up and look at her. It's supercool and I'm just so proud."

The meeting must have been a true motivator for Caitlin, because it was in this game that she went on to break Pete Maravich's record and become the all-time NCAA scoring champ for both women and men.

WHO IS YOUR

role model? What is it about them that is so inspiring to you? What would it mean to you to meet them in person? What would you say?

ELITE
EIGHT

The Hawkeyes finished second in the conference regular season standings. For the third year in a row, they won the Big Ten tournament. They earned a number-one seed as they headed into the NCAA tournament and then quickly defeated Holy Cross, West Virginia, and Colorado.

On April 1, 2024, the Hawkeyes would play last season's defending champion, the LSU Tigers. Once again, they'd be playing against star players like Angel Reese, Hailey Van Lith, Flau'jae Johnson, Mikaylah Williams, and Aneesah Morrow. The year before, the matchup had drawn a record 9.9 million viewers. In 2024, it was a record 16.1 million. The game became ESPN's best audience for a college basketball game ever, of men's and women's games.

The game was tied at 45 at the half, and then Caitlin started showing just why she was considered an all-time scoring leader. She hit deep three-pointer after three-pointer, bringing the score to 61–52. She hit her 9th of the game, also her 62nd March Madness three-pointer. This shot broke a new record, making her the all-time leader of three-point shots during the women's NCAA tournament, breaking Diana Taurasi's previous record. This brought the score to 80–69 with five minutes and five seconds left on the clock. As she ran down the court, she pumped her chest and cheered along with the crowd.

This time, Iowa got the results they were hoping for. Caitlin Clark led Iowa back to the Final Four, scoring 41 points in a 94–87 win.

For the second straight year, they were headed to the NCAA Final Four, where Iowa would be facing off against the University of Connecticut, while North Carolina State played South Carolina. More buzz and excitement about women's NCAA basketball was brewing than ever before.

"The NCAA got it right," NBA legend Magic Johnson tweeted. "Because tonight's women's tournament matchups are one of the best in history! As a basketball fan and a fan of women's sports, this is heaven for me!"

After a rough first half in the Iowa/UConn Final Four game, Caitlin scored 21 points, leading her team to a 71–69 win over UConn. And with this win, the Hawkeyes were off to the National Championship once again.

A SECOND CHANCE

The 2024 NCAA Division I tournament set viewing records in all rounds. An average of 18.7 million TV viewers watched on ABC and ESPN. This was 89 percent higher than the year before. At a record high, the women's NCAA Championship game peaked at 24 million viewers. It was the most-watched basketball game in the country since 2019—not only for college women's teams, but also for men's, in both college and pro teams.

The **South Carolina Gamecocks** referred to their matchup with Iowa as their "revenge tour." The previous season, South Carolina had been undefeated—until the 2023 national semifinals, when the Hawkeyes came out victorious, winning 77–73 and bumping South Carolina out of the competition. Now, South Carolina wanted revenge and had their eye on the prize.

But Iowa was ready to fight for it, too. The Hawkeyes started out strong with a quick 10–0 lead over the Gamecocks. Caitlin scored 18 points in the first quarter, setting a championship game record for most points in a single period. She would go on to score 30 points against South Carolina, bringing her career total to 3,951.

Iowa had a strong game, but South Carolina was hard to beat. After the first quarter, they put five defenders on Caitlin, including South Carolina guard Raven Johnson. With Raven as her primary defender, Caitlin scored only 12 points over the final three quarters. In addition to South Carolina's strong defense, there was 6-foot-7 South Carolina center Kamilla Cardoso, who snagged 17 rebounds and earned the title of Most Outstanding Player.

In the end, South Carolina won the game, beating Iowa 87–75. In doing so, South Carolina became only the fifth women's basketball program in history to record a "perfect season," going undefeated through the regular season and all the way to the championship. For the Hawkeyes, though, it was another heartbreaking loss.

2X NATIONAL RUNNER-UP

The Hawkeyes cried together in the locker room, comforting one another. This loss was especially tough. This was the last time Caitlin would play in an Iowa jersey—the last game of her NCAA career. Of course, she had wanted to finish her college career with a championship medal—a storybook ending—but it hadn't happened that way.

Still, there was so much to celebrate. "I'm proud of my team," Coach Bluder said in a post-game press conference. "Finishing national runner-up two years in a row was an amazing feat. . . . I know we're going to look back on this and be very, very proud of the effort we gave this year."

And while Caitlin was sad, she also felt proud of herself and of her team for all they had achieved. "At the end of the day people aren't going to remember how many points I scored," she said. "That's not going to matter to people in the end. I hope they remember how we made them feel, how we brought joy to their lives, how we gave their families something to scream about on the TV on the weekends. I hope those are the biggest things people remember."

CRUSHING IT

Caitlin continued to rack up the awards and set new records during her senior year. Here are just some of her awards and achievements:

★ Iowa's all-time leading scorer
★ Most 30-point games by any man or woman in Division I in the past 25 seasons
★ Big Ten's all-time leader in assists
★ Iowa's all-time leader in assists
★ Big Ten Player of the Week conference record
★ Big Ten all-time scoring record
★ Division I women's career scoring leader
★ Iowa's single-game scoring record breaker
★ All-time leader in points among major women's college basketball players
★ Big Ten career record for three-pointers
★ NCAA single-season record for three-pointers
★ All-time NCAA Division I men's and women's scoring leader
★ Unanimous Big Ten Player of the Year
★ Most three-pointers in a single season by any male or female Division I player
★ The first Division I women's player to score at least 1,000 points in two different seasons
★ First player in NCAA tournament history with three career 40-point games

Back on campus, Caitlin and her teammates were honored in a celebration commemorating the Hawkeyes' second consecutive national runner-up finish in the NCAA tournament. Caitlin looked around at the 8,000 fans crowded into the Carver-Hawkeye Arena, a stadium she had come to know so well. She loved her fans more than anything. She had developed a deep and sincere appreciation for every player on the Hawkeyes. She'd built an irreplaceable bond with her coaches.

Caitlin had tears in her eyes when Iowa's athletic director announced that the Hawkeyes would be retiring her number 22 jersey. This meant that no one would ever wear that number on the Iowa team again, as a way to honor Caitlin Clark's massive impact on the sport. Only three other jerseys had been retired like this in the history of the program. At the announcement, the crowd stood, cheering and whistling.

"I would say you've all inspired me as much as I inspired you," Caitlin said to her adoring fans. "You allowed me to live out my dream every single day, and for that, I'm very thankful. It's been very special, and this place will always be home to me."

INDIANA FEVER

O**n an evening in April 2024,** Caitlin Clark was at the Brooklyn Academy of Music, awaiting the WNBA Draft. Alongside the other new and incoming WNBA players, she waited to find out which team would pick her.

Meanwhile, over 6,000 fans had crowded into the Gainbridge Fieldhouse in downtown Indianapolis. This was home court for their WNBA team, the Indiana Fever. They were about to watch the live broadcast of the WNBA Draft on a big screen, to find out which players the team would pick for the next season. Some people had driven five hours from Iowa to Indiana to watch the live coverage. In December 2023, the Indiana Fever had won the draft lottery, meaning they would get the first pick on which player would join their team.

Three Indiana players sat next to each other on the sidelines: Erica Wheeler, Lexie Hull, and Maya Caldwell. Erica, who had been the veteran point guard who started in all 40 games for the Fever the previous season, leaned forward with her hands on her teammates' knees, awaiting the announcement.

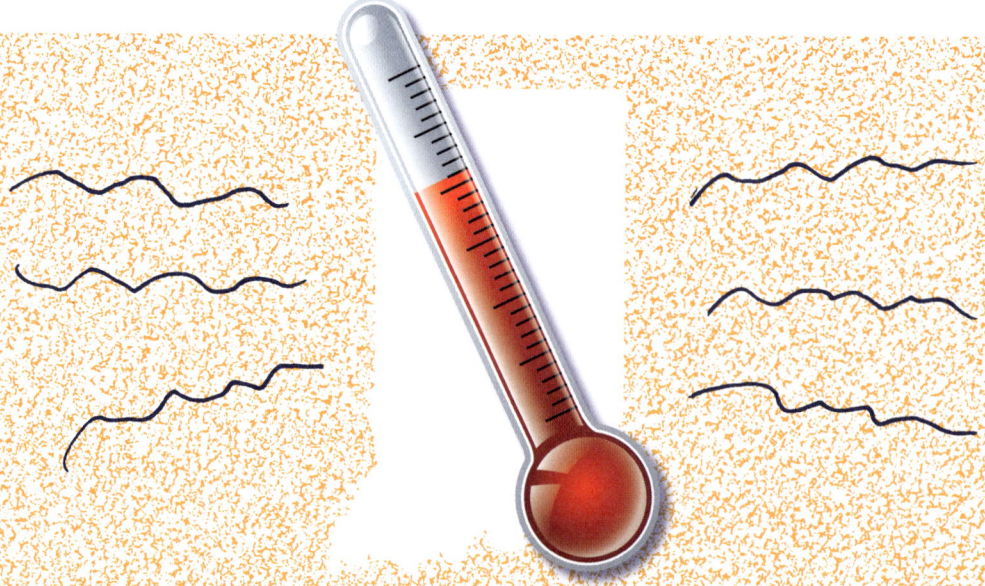

"The first pick in the 2024 WNBA Draft, the Indiana Fever selects . . .
Caitlin Clark!"

At the sound of Caitlin's name, the three women leapt from their seats in celebration. They all had one of Caitlin's red number 22 jerseys and they slipped the shirts on over their heads and cheered. Balloons fell from the ceiling and the crowd went wild.

On the screen, Caitlin held up an Indiana Fever jersey and posed for photographs.

"I can't think of a better place for myself to start my career," Caitlin said later in a press conference. "A place that loves basketball, supports women's basketball, and an organization that really does things the right way."

She was also honored to receive such a warm welcome from incredible players. Erica Wheeler had reached out to Caitlin on social media, letting her know she would love to mentor her and give advice whenever she needed it. Caitlin described Erica as "somebody that's been having my back and we're not even really teammates yet."

CATCHING THE
FEVER

t was a quick turnaround from the end of Caitlin's NCAA career to the start of her WNBA season—no time to rest. Before she knew it, she was driving up to the Gainbridge Fieldhouse in her new home city of Indianapolis, about to play her first preseason home game in the WNBA. She barely had time to think about how she had made it to the WNBA, fulfilling that dream she had written on a piece of paper in third grade.

It was a rainy day in May, but fans swarmed the stadium. There were 13,000 people there to see the teams play, an incredible number of people to see a game before the regular season had even begun. They had to open the third floor of seats at the Fieldhouse to accommodate everyone.

Tunnel WALK

The WNBA "tunnel walk" has become a fashion runway event. When players make their first appearance at games, they enter through the concrete tunnel that connects the locker room to the arena, and they make those entrances in style. Athletes get the chance to show off their personal styles and individuality, which is something they don't get to do in their uniforms on the court.

With the new attention on women's teams, fashion and designer brands like Balmain, Prada, and Versace are jumping at the chance to have athletes show off their outfits. This also helps players get media attention and build their platforms.

Caitlin was treated like a celebrity, escorted into the stadium by security. She was dressed up for the tunnel walk in a white turtleneck, loose white pants, and white sneakers. There were so many kids wearing number 22 jerseys, screaming her name. This was what it was all about.

When Caitlin made her first basket on a driving layup, the crowd whooped and cheered. She went on to nail a three-pointer from behind the arc. NaLyssa Smith led the Fever with 21 points and 6 rebounds. Caitlin finished the game with 12 points, 8 rebounds, and 6 assists. Aliyah Boston and Katie Lou Samuelson finished with 11 points each. The Indiana Fever came out with an 83–80 victory over the Atlanta Dream.

After the game, Caitlin went right up to the stands to sign autographs. A crowd of kids was waiting patiently behind the gate, holding signs, basketballs, or their shirts. Caitlin went down the line signing as many autographs as she could, giving hugs, and taking pictures. Her hand got tired from all the writing, and she loved every minute of it.

But the start of her WNBA career was not perfectly smooth. In her debut game against the Connecticut Sun, Caitlin did score an impressive 20 points, which made her the second-highest-scoring player in a Fever debut game—but unfortunately, she also had 10 turnovers. This set a record for the most turnovers in a WNBA debut, which was not a good look. Indiana lost this game 92–71.

Caitlin struggled in the second game of the season as well, scoring only 9 points. It was a home game against the New York Liberty. There was a massive crowd of 17,274 people there to watch. A few times, after Caitlin missed a shot, she brought her hands to her head in frustration.

Caitlin would have to get used to the pace of the game in the WNBA. The plays moved a lot faster than they had in college, switching from offense to defense and

back again at lightning speed. She would also have to adapt to the physicality of a professional game. The players knocked each other around, and the refs didn't call as many fouls as they did in the NCAA. Caitlin got pushed and shoved, causing her to turn over the ball. On the court, she showed her annoyance, pleading with the refs when she thought they had missed a call. When she got angry or frustrated after missing a shot, she threw the ball out of bounds or slammed her fist into the padding around the stanchion (the pole that holds up the basketball net). The refs blew the whistle, calling technical fouls on her.

Caitlin may have been a newbie and a rookie, but she was there to win, and her fiery side sometimes came out. In some ways, she was even more competitive now than she had been in college. The stakes were incredibly high, and so was the pressure. This was her job now. She needed to show that she belonged here on this court. She would need to acclimate to this game and figure out how to manage her frustration—not to extinguish her fire, but to learn how to channel it. She had to prove herself.

CHEMISTRY ON
THE COURT

—

oach Christie Sides wanted to help Caitlin put her passion to good use, rather than expending unnecessary energy on getting mad at the refs. She had a message for Caitlin: "Empower your teammates." The coach saw that the Fever could be a powerhouse team if they figured out how to work together. They all had to get to know each other better, learn how to lean on each other, and determine how to read each other and communicate on the court.

That message really resonated with Caitlin. Empowering her teammates meant giving them opportunities to shine and setting them up for success. They were in it together. When times were tough, Caitlin learned she could count on her teammates to lift her up, and she could do the same for them.

She had teammates like Erica Wheeler and Lexie Hull who had outwardly shown their support for Caitlin from the moment she was drafted on the team. Aliyah Boston, the 6-foot-5 Fever forward, was there to give Caitlin a pep talk as they walked together off the court at halftime at Caitlin's less-than-perfect debut, reminding Caitlin that her teammates had her back, and that your rookie year in the WNBA was supposed to be an adjustment period. There was NaLyssa Smith, a dynamic forward and center with incredible rebounding skills and a strong offense. Caitlin could also count on Fever guard Kelsey Mitchell, an incredibly talented player. Caitlin and Kelsey had the potential to become a power duo if they could just find their rhythm.

Gradually, the team started to gel. Caitlin and Kelsey Mitchell started developing their connection, learning how to read each other and make great plays. They also started to really appreciate each other's strengths: Caitlin with her quick, smart passes and Kelsey with her speed, intuition, and consistency when it came to finishing at the rim.

"Basketball is a language," Kelsey said in a postgame interview. And referring to Caitlin Clark as "C-Squared," she said, "You gotta get on the same page with your counterparts. I think me and C-Squared like to play a certain way and that's fast and up-tempo, so I'm gonna always align [with her] based on how she's playing and how the game is going."

Caitlin also noticed what was happening between her and Kelsey on the court. "You can see us develop our chemistry more and more. . . . She's starting to read my eyes and see what I want in transition. It's created a lot of fun plays for us."

Very soon, Caitlin and Kelsey were speaking the same language—a language of their own. The "backcourt duo" was unstoppable in a game against the Phoenix Mercury on August 16, 2024. Caitlin recorded a double-double, scoring 29 points and 10 assists, including 4 three-pointers. Kelsey scored 28 points of her own—18 of them from three-pointers—as well as 5 rebounds.

But the magic was truly in the way they fed off each other. Caitlin dribbled down court with two defenders on her and launched the ball between them to what looked like empty space. Kelsey seemed to appear out of thin air, snatching the ball and heading to the net for an easy layup. The defenders turned around, not even aware yet of what had happened behind their backs. Fans were in awe as they watched Caitlin's "insane dime" to Kelsey.

That day, they landed a 98–89 win over the Mercury, legend Diana Taurasi's team.

In the next game, against the Seattle Storm, Caitlin broke yet another record, becoming the WNBA's all-time leader for assists in a season by a rookie. She did it in the third quarter of the game, a beautiful full-court assist to Kelsey.

"I want to set my teammates up first and foremost," Caitlin said, "because that's going to help you have the most successful team."

Despite her few early rough patches, it didn't take long for Caitlin to prove that she belonged in the WNBA. She had a historic rookie season. In her first six games in the league, she averaged 12 points and 6 assists per game. By that July, she was averaging 20 points and 12 assists per game.

By September 2024, she had already broken a number of records for the WNBA. Caitlin was named the WNBA Rookie of the Month for May, July, and August, joining star player Aliyah Boston as the only other rookie in WNBA history to receive this recognition multiple times. Caitlin became the fastest rookie in WNBA history to record at least 400 points and 200 assists. She became the only WNBA rookie to record a triple-double (which she did twice), and she had the most double-doubles by a guard in the league in a rookie season. She led the league in assists, points scored, and three-pointers per game. In a matchup against the Las Vegas Aces on September 13, 2024, she hit yet another big milestone. Caitlin earned the title of the WNBA all-time leader in assists for a single season after passing the ball to **Kelsey Mitchell**, who made a quick drive to the basket to score.

Caitlin's presence on the Fever also helped to set records in the WNBA for TV viewership and attendance at games. She received the most fan All-Star votes in WNBA history with over 700,000 votes, despite being a rookie. And Caitlin was selected alongside Fever center Aliyah Boston and guard Kelsey Mitchell to the WNBA All-Star game.

And an incredibly impressive feat: Caitlin led the Indiana Fever back to the playoffs for the first time since 2016!

On October 3, 2024, the WNBA commissioner called Coach Sides to share some important news, and Caitlin and her Fever teammates gathered around to listen. "Is Caitlin Clark in the room?" the commissioner asked. "It feels like just yesterday when I called your name to the stage as the number one pick in this year's draft and you held the Indiana Fever jersey for the first time. And what a record-breaking season for you and the entire team full of outstanding performances. I know all of you had hard work and dedication and it's paid off. . . . and I know the best is yet to come. So, congratulations, Caitlin. You are the 2024 Kia WNBA Rookie of the Year."

At this announcement, Caitlin's teammates jumped up and down around her, cheering and congratulating her.

The award meant a lot to Caitlin, and in typical Caitlin fashion, she was already thinking about the work she was ready to do with her team to achieve even more the following season. The season was a massive success, but the Fever were knocked out of the playoffs by the Connecticut Sun in game two of the first round. Caitlin couldn't wait to see how far they could go next time around.

"The fun part is I feel like I'm just scratching the surface," Caitlin told ESPN. "I know there's a lot of room for me to continue to improve. So that's what excites me the most. I feel like I could continue to get a lot better, and before we know it, I'm sure we'll all be back here and ready for the next year."

All-Star Game

The All-Star Game, held on July 20, 2024, at Phoenix's Footprint Center in Arizona, featured top league players chosen by fan votes, coaches, and media. The matchup showcased the US national team (Team USA), who would soon head to the Paris Olympics, versus the WNBA All-Stars (Team WNBA). Both teams boasted major stars, including Caitlin Clark, Diana Taurasi, Nneka Ogwumike, Brittney Griner, Breanna Stewart, Kelsey Plum, A'ja Wilson, Jackie Young, Sabrina Ionescu, and Aliyah Boston. The game drew a record audience, with a sold-out crowd and 3.4 million viewers, surpassing previous records.

Rookies Caitlin Clark of the Fever and Angel Reese of the Chicago Sky had stellar performances. Despite a quiet scoring night, Caitlin set a rookie record with 10 assists and Angel was second in rebounds.

Early in the third quarter, Caitlin drove toward the net, faking out her defenders and sent the ball to Angel Reese with a no-look pass. Angel was in perfect position and received the ball for a quick layup. The two players high-fived while running back to defense.

Caitlin also made an astounding assist to her Fever teammate Aliyah Boston. She passed the ball through the narrow space between her opponents and her teammate, landing the ball right into Aliyah's hands for a basket.

Team WNBA pulled off the win against Team USA, 117-109—a tough loss for the Olympians. But they did manage to bounce back and win the gold medal in Paris just a few weeks later.

Caitlin and Angel are looking forward to playing together in the years to come. "Hopefully in four years we'll be Olympians together," Angel said.

IMPACTS ON WOMEN'S
BASKETBALL

One of the greatest impacts Caitlin Clark has had is on women's basketball itself. Because of The Caitlin Clark Effect, more people are tuning in to women's basketball than ever before. That includes not only your typical sports fan, but also casual sports fans—and even people who don't usually watch sports at all. Caitlin has also inspired the next generation to get out there and play.

"I'm all about growing the women's game," Caitlin said in a press conference. "And I'm glad I've given something that little girls can scream about at the top of their lungs . . . when I was younger, I was doing the exact same thing."

No one knows what the next few years will bring for Caitlin Clark, but she will undoubtedly continue breaking records, rising to new heights, and pushing herself to be the best that she can be. One of her greatest traits is her ability to stay grounded, even with all the fame and hype buzzing around her.

Caitlin will never forget what it felt like to be that kid from Iowa with a big dream. She will never forget what it felt like to work for it, practicing for hours on end in her driveway, chasing her brothers, just trying to keep up and refusing to lose, and waiting in line at the stadium holding out a jersey to her favorite player for an autograph. These memories motivate and inspire her every day to be the incredible basketball player and the amazing person she has become.

Basketball is one of Caitlin's favorite things in the world, but what matters to her most is that she can continue to inspire people to make their dreams a reality. She thinks about her legacy, or how she wants people to think of her and remember her long after her time on the court. She doesn't want people to only remember how many points she scored, how many records she broke, or how many games she won. "I hope it's what I was able to do for the game of women's basketball," she said in a press conference. "I hope it is the young boys and young girls that are inspired to play this sport or dream to do whatever they want to do in their lives . . . because all you have to do is dream."

Philanthropy
off the Court

At Iowa, Caitlin majored in marketing and minored in communications, an education she could apply to her basketball brand. She started the Caitlin Clark Foundation, with a mission to "uplift and improve the lives of youth and their communities through education, nutrition, and sport—three pillars Caitlin believes were foundational in her success." Through the foundation, Caitlin took on initiatives such as the Warm Up Clothing, Gear Up Sports Equipment, and Fuel Up and Stock Up Food Pantry Campaigns. She also set out to address food scarcity in the community where she grew up in Iowa, partnering with local food banks like the Coralville Food Pantry, helping to organize food drives, and fundraising to help the nonprofit carry out its mission.

CHAPTER

6

ALL ABOUT
CAITLIN

FULL COURT FACTS

Caitlin Clark is all about basketball most of the time, but she does also have other hobbies and interests that make her unique! Here are some fast facts about the basketball superstar to help us get to know her even better.

Favorite Singer

Caitlin Clark likes to blast music on her headphones to pump her up before a game. Her favorite artist of all time? Country singer Luke Combs, who congratulated Caitlin on the day of the WNBA Draft.

Caitlin Is a Swiftie

Another of Caitlin's favorite musicians is Taylor Swift, and the two icons have some things in common, including their fan bases (Clarkies and Swifties unite!) and their effects on American culture. Caitlin's favorite Taylor Swift song is "Enchanted," from the album *Speak Now*. It was the song she played to celebrate being the number one pick of the WNBA, "even though it's kind of a sad song," Caitlin said.

Caitlin's Golden Retriever

Caitlin loves her pup, a golden retriever named Bella. Before the first day of her sophomore year at Iowa, Caitlin and Bella sat posed for a picture with "First Day of School" signs. Caitlin's major: business. Bella's major: napping. Caitlin's hobby: Candy Crush. Bella's hobby: walking. Caitlin wrote, "I am 6 ft. 0 in. tall" and for Bella, "2 ft. 0 in." Caitlin still holds onto a life-sized cardboard cutout of Bella from the COVID-19 days, when only close family were allowed in the seats. Her mom brought the cutout of Bella to fill an empty seat and cheer Caitlin on.

Gamer

Video games were just one of the things Caitlin and her brothers used to argue about in the basement when they were kids. Before the start of her WNBA season, Caitlin confirmed that she brought her PS5 with her to a hotel where she was staying before her first pro game, but she didn't get a chance to use it. "I watch movies and I have my PS5 with me," she said. "But I haven't hooked it up or played it at all. Taking a few naps. That's about it."

Baking

One of the hobbies that helps Caitlin relax in the offseason is baking, an activity that she and her mom have always liked to do together. Brownies are one of her favorite things to bake, and one of her favorite sweets to eat is warm chocolate chip cookies. Her mom, Anne, often brings a dessert to share when she comes to watch Caitlin play, which goes over pretty well with the team.

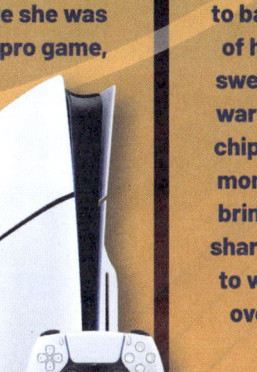

Golf

In the offseason, Caitlin likes to spend her time on the golf course. Her dad first got her into the sport. For one of her birthdays as a kid, her parents gifted her pink clubs and a pink bag. She has fond memories of golfing with her dad and older brother. In college, she found that some of her teammates, coaches, and the team manager played golf. Over the summer, they would play twilight golf, out there swinging until the sun went down.

Astrological Sign

Caitlin's birthday is January 22, which makes her an Aquarius. In astrology, those born under the sign of Aquarius are said to be creative, generous, intelligent, and independent, as well as stubborn at times and sometimes wary of authority. They are also said to be natural leaders who thrive on teamwork and are committed to making the world a better place.

Favorite Movie

Caitlin shared her favorite movie on a Fever social media post: 1998's *The Parent Trap*. The film is about childhood innocence, the importance of family, loss and reunion, and having fun—themes that must resonate with our basketball superstar.

Favorite Foods

In her days as a Hawkeye, Caitlin ate like a college kid. For breakfast, she'd enjoy a fast-food bacon, egg, and cheese sandwich with an elaborate coffee drink like an iced macchiato with vanilla sweet cream cold foam. Before a game, she liked to load up on packaged snacks that have a healthy portion of carbohydrates, and at halftime, she'd refuel with a quick snack, like an apple sauce packet. Her favorite post-game meal was "chicken parm, pasta, and a big glass of chocolate milk." To satisfy her sweet tooth, she indulged in warm chocolate chip cookies (best if they were homemade in her mother's kitchen). Her favorite ice cream flavor is coffee.

Big Bro

Caitlin and her big brother Blake share a deep bond rooted in sports. When she needs someone to lift her up, Blake's the person she'll call. Caitlin appreciates Blake's insights, saying, "He knows the game really, really well. I can lean on him after tough games." But their connection goes beyond sports. "I talk to him every day, whether it's about basketball, school, or life. He's always there for me!"

Favorite MLB Team

Caitlin is a pro at nearly everything she does, but after trying her hand at being a sports commentator, she discovered it might not be her strong suit. Her Fever teammate, Lexi Hull, secretly filmed and posted a video of Caitlin pretending to announce the play-by-play of a Phillies game from their hotel room, and the video went viral. In a press conference, Caitlin told reporters, "I've been following the Phillies, so I kind of know some of their players and stuff. It was pretty funny. I messed up a few times. That's a hard gig."

Funny Person

As Caitlin has gotten more comfortable with her Fever teammates, her personality and sense of humor have come out. Coach Sides described Caitlin off court as "a really funny person with a quick wit." In a press conference, Caitlin attributed some of her humor to a Halloween tradition in her hometown of Des Moines, Iowa, in which trick-or-treaters are required to tell a joke to earn their candy. Every Halloween, her mom writes down a list of the jokes the kids tell her at the door and shares them with Caitlin and her brothers. "Other than that," Caitlin said, "I'm just a sarcastic person."

WHICH SPORT IS RIGHT FOR YOU?

1 What type of physical activity do you enjoy the most?
- A) High-intensity and fast-paced
- B) Strategic and team-oriented
- C) Individual and skill-based
- D) Endurance-building
- E) Creative and expressive

2 How do you prefer to interact with others in a sport?
- A) Competing directly against opponents
- B) Collaborating closely with teammates
- C) Performing individually but still part of a team
- D) Building personal endurance and self-discipline
- E) Showcasing artistic or acrobatic skills

3 What motivates you the most?
- A) Adrenaline and excitement
- B) Team success and strategy
- C) Personal improvement and mastery
- D) Long-term goals and personal growth
- E) Creativity and artistic expression

4 What's your preferred environment for sports?

A) Outdoors or in a dynamic, fast-paced, high-energy setting

B) In a team setting with structured practices

C) On a field or court where you can focus on personal technique

D) On a track or meditative setting where you can focus on gradual progress

E) On a stage or field where you can perform and showcase

5 How do you handle competition?

A) You love high-stakes, competitive scenarios

B) You enjoy strategizing with a team and working toward a common goal

C) You like to focus on personal achievement and developing your skills

D) You embrace challenges as a way for you to build your resilience and stamina

E) You like to blend performance with competition in a creative way

Results Key

Mostly As: High-Energy Team Sports
Recommended sports: Soccer, Basketball, Rugby, Ice Hockey
Why: You thrive on fast-paced, competitive environments and enjoy the thrill of direct competition.

Mostly Bs: Team Strategy Sports
Recommended sports: Football, Volleyball, Baseball, Water Polo
Why: You appreciate strategic gameplay and working closely with teammates to achieve success.

Mostly Cs: Individual Skill Sports
Recommended sports: Tennis, Golf, Martial Arts, Swimming
Why: You enjoy focusing on personal skill development

and performance, with a mix of individual effort and team context.

Mostly Ds: Endurance and Long-Distance Sports
Recommended sports: Running, Cycling, Rowing, Triathlon
Why: You are motivated by long-term goals and enjoy building endurance and personal resilience.

Mostly Es: Creative and Artistic Sports
Recommended sports: Gymnastics, Figure Skating, Dance, Cheerleading
Why: You enjoy showcasing creativity and expressiveness through your sport, with a focus on performance and artistry.

Defensive Strategies Against Caitlin

If you happen to find yourself in a position where you're defending Caitlin Clark (hey, it could happen!), here are a few strategies you can use:

- Put the pressure on her as soon as she catches the ball. Force her to drive and dribble rather than shooting.

- Get on her right-hand side after she passes the half-court line. She's got what it takes to sink three-pointers from anywhere on the court, so you'll want to cover her even when she's seemingly miles from the basket.

- Be consistent and physical, showing her you're confident enough to stop her.

- Show no fear and stay tough!

Learn How to Be a Playmaker Like Caitlin

Caitlin's exceptional playmaking skills are based on a few key concepts and fundamentals that can elevate any player's game. Here's a breakdown of some of her skills and moves to help you play like she does:

Constant Scanning

- **Vision:** Caitlin keeps her eyes up and constantly scans the floor, mapping out the position of teammates and defenders even before she receives the ball.

- **Sneaking a peek:** Before her hands touch the ball, she sneaks a glance down the court to assess the situation, allowing her to make precise passes.

On-Target Passing

- **Accuracy:** She delivers passes with pinpoint accuracy, often finding teammates from long distances and through tight defenses.

- **One-handed passes:** Caitlin executes one-handed passes effectively, which shows her skill and precision.

Using Court Space

- **Deep shooting:** She takes long three-pointers, drawing defenders and opening up the court for her teammates.

- **Kicking ahead:** She often "kicks" or pushes the ball ahead quickly, avoiding extra dribbles to find teammates in stride and create easy scoring opportunities.

Changing Speed

- **Manipulating defense:** Caitlin varies her speed to keep defenders off-balance, slowing down or using sudden bursts of speed to find defensive gaps.

Engaging Defenders

- **Drawing defenders:** She engages and draws in defenders, making it seem as if she's driving toward the basket, which leaves her teammates open. Then she passes the ball instead for them to finish the play with a shot.

- **Anticipation:** Caitlin passes to where her teammates are going rather than where they are. By anticipating her teammates' movements, she is able to accurately get the ball into their hands.

Skillful Playmaking

- **Touch and timing:** Her passes are not only accurate but also delivered with the right touch and at the right time.

Vision Foundation

- **Court vision:** A strong foundation in court vision allows her to make high-quality passes without needing extra dribbles.

Credit: Techniques discussed are based on insights from Sam Allen, a coach from PGC (Point Guard College), a program that offers basketball camps for dedicated players from fourth grade to college.

WNBA
CHAMPS

Since its inception in 1997, the WNBA has featured some of the greatest athletes in women's basketball history. Here's a look at the WNBA champions throughout the years:

2024 | New York Liberty defeated Minnesota Lynx 3-2.

2023 | Las Vegas Aces defeated New York Liberty 3-1.

2022 | Las Vegas Aces defeated Connecticut Sun 3-1.

2021 | Chicago Sky defeated Phoenix Mercury 3-1.

2020 | Seattle Storm defeated Las Vegas Aces 3-0.

2019 | Washington Mystics defeated Connecticut Sun 3-2.

2018 | Seattle Storm defeated Washington Mystics 3-0.

2017 | Minnesota Lynx defeated Los Angeles Sparks 3-2.

2016 | Los Angeles Sparks defeated Minnesota Lynx 3-2.

2015 | Minnesota Lynx defeated Indiana Fever 3-2.

2014 | Phoenix Mercury defeated Chicago Sky 3-0.

2013 | **Minnesota Lynx** defeated Atlanta Dream 3-0.

2012 | **Indiana Fever** defeated Minnesota Lynx 3-1.

2011 | **Minnesota Lynx** defeated Atlanta Dream 3-0.

2010 | **Seattle Storm** defeated Atlanta Dream 3-0.

2009 | **Phoenix Mercury** defeated Indiana Fever 3-2.

2008 | **Detroit Shock** defeated San Antonio Silver Stars 3-0.

2007 | **Phoenix Mercury** defeated Detroit Shock 3-2.

2006 | **Detroit Shock** defeated Sacramento Monarchs 3-2.

2005 | **Sacramento Monarchs** defeated Connecticut Sun 3-1.

2004 | **Seattle Storm** defeated Connecticut Sun 2-1.

2003 | **Detroit Shock** defeated Los Angeles Sparks 2-1.

2002 | **Los Angeles Sparks** defeated New York Liberty 2-0.

2001 | **Los Angeles Sparks** defeated Charlotte Sting 2-0.

2000 | **Houston Comets** defeated New York Liberty 2-0.

1999 | **Houston Comets** defeated New York Liberty 2-1.

1998 | **Houston Comets** defeated Phoenix Mercury 2-1.

1997 | **Houston Comets** defeated New York Liberty 1-0.

MOST VALUABLE
PLAYER

At the end of every season, a panel of sportswriters and broadcasters vote to determine who will receive the annual Most Valuable Player (MVP) Award. The award goes to some of the most talented, dedicated and hardest working players, and those who have made a significant impact on the sport. Here's a list of MVP award winners over the years:

2024 | **A'ja Wilson**, Las Vegas Aces

2023 | **Breanna Stewart**, New York Liberty

2022 | **A'ja Wilson**, Las Vegas Aces

2021 | **Jonquel Jones**, Connecticut Sun

2020 | **A'ja Wilson**, Las Vegas Aces

2019 | **Elena Delle Donne**, Washington Mystics

2018 | **Breanna Stewart**, Seattle Storm

2017 | **Sylvia Fowles**, Minnesota Lynx

2016 | **Nneka Ogwumike**, Los Angeles Sparks

2015 | **Elena Delle Donne**, Chicago Sky

2014 | **Maya Moore**, Minnesota Lynx

2013 | **Candace Parker**, Los Angeles Sparks

2012 | **Tina Charles**, Connecticut Sun

2011 | **Tamika Catchings**, Indiana Fever

2010 | **Lauren Jackson**, Seattle Storm

2009 | **Diana Taurasi**, Phoenix Mercury

2008 | **Candace Parker**, Los Angeles Sparks

2007 | **Lauren Jackson**, Seattle Storm

2006 | **Lisa Leslie**, Los Angeles Sparks

2005 | **Sheryl Swoopes**, Houston Comets

2004 | **Lisa Leslie**, Los Angeles Sparks

2003 | **Lauren Jackson**, Seattle Storm

2002 | **Sheryl Swoopes**, Houston Comets

2001 | **Lisa Leslie**, Los Angeles Sparks

2000 | **Sheryl Swoopes**, Houston Comets

1999 | **Yolanda Griffith**, Sacramento Monarchs

1998 | **Cynthia Cooper**, Houston Comets

1997 | **Cynthia Cooper**, Houston Comets

PHOTO CREDITS

ACKNOWLEDGMENTS

I loved living inside the world of Caitlin Clark as I wrote this book. I hope that reading about her talent, persistence, and determination will inspire you as much as she has inspired me. If you have a dream and a passion, work hard and go after it! And make sure to lean on those who are there to support you along the way.

I would like to thank the team of people who have been there to support me on my journey. Thank you to my editors at Quarto, Katie McGuire and Nicole James, for their guidance and feedback. Thanks to my friends and readers of my work over the years, fellow artists in the Cut and Paste ARIM (Artist Residency in Motherhood), and my writing teachers at Sarah Lawrence College, Tufts, and Friends School. Thank you to my writing buddies who are in it with me—Nicole Haroutunian, Jocelyn Jane Cox, and so many others. Thanks to my parents, Jan and Michael, my sister, Rachel, and to my incredible network of family and friends. I will always be grateful to my husband, Kevin, and my daughters, Nora and Rosie. They are the very best.

ABOUT THE AUTHOR

SARA WEISS holds an MFA from Sarah Lawrence College. She is the author of three books about the endearing qualities of dogs: *A Frenchie Life*, *A Golden Life*, and *A Labrador Life*. Her writing has also appeared in journals and magazines such as *Literary Mama*, *Mutha*, *Lilith*, *Waterwheel Review*, *Bustle*, and *Brain Child*, among others. She has written audio scripts for *Good Night Stories for Rebel Girls* and works as a college writing consultant. She lives in the Hudson Valley with her husband, two daughters, and their smallish dog.

© 2025 by Quarto Publishing Group USA Inc.

First published in 2025 by becker&mayer!kids, an imprint of The Quarto Group,
142 West 36th Street, 4th Floor, New York, NY 10018, USA
(212) 779-4972 • www.Quarto.com

becker&mayer!kids titles are also available at discount for retail, wholesale,
promotional, and bulk purchase. For details, contact the Special Sales Manager by
email at specialsales@quarto.com or by mail at The Quarto Group, Attn: Special
Sales Manager, 100 Cummings Center Suite 265D, Beverly, MA 01915 USA.

10 9 8 7 6 5 4 3 2 1

ISBN: 978-0-7603-9683-4

Digital edition published in 2025
eISBN: 978-0-7603-9684-1

Library of Congress Control Number: 2024949399

Group Publisher: Rage Kindelsperger
Creative Director: Laura Drew
Managing Editor: Cara Donaldson
Editors: Katie McGuire, Nicole James
Text: Sara Weiss
Cover Illustrator: Jamie Coe
Cover Design: Scott Richardson
Interior Design: Brad Norr Design

Printed in China

Lexile® 1070L